THE TWINS

Michael Minicky

THE TWINS

Copyright © 2022

All Rights Reserved

ISBN: 978-1-958332-00-9

MICHAEL MINICKY

This book is dedicated to my daughter Catti-Brie who is the ***Light*** that keeps my ***Darkness*** away.

Table of Contents

Prelude 1

Chapter 1 Another Day 8

Chapter 2 A Message Delivered 21

Chapter 3 The Funeral 42

Chapter 4 What the Heart Wants 57

Chapter 5 Betsy's Nightlight 82

Chapter 6 Messages 111

Chapter 7 Aubrey's 133

Chapter 8 Frightening Clues and More! 151

Chapter 9 Wrong Place, Wrong Time 173

Chapter 10 Claire Visits Detective Marshall 189

Chapter 11 Lisa and Lucy Want to Play 217

Epilogue 250

MICHAEL MINICKY

Page left blank intentionally.

MICHAEL MINICKY

Prelude

Detective Marshal lit up a cigarette, took a long, deep drag, and then closed his eyes while slowly letting out the inhaled smoke. He was a big man with a boxer's build, although, in the last couple of years, he had found it harder and harder to go to the gym, and so a small belly had started to show. He was in his early forties, but the grey forming in his hair, the deep lines on his face, and the black patches under his eyes made him look more like he was in his fifties. That is the price one pays when they become a homicide detective—the killing never stops.

He was on his 5th homicide case for the day. But again, what do you expect when you live in a big city like St. Louis—one of the most dangerous cities in America? The detective remembered the time when he had first gotten into homicide. He was so young and naive; he had thought it would be just like it was always on TV. He would show up to a crime scene, piece clues together, and then nab the bad guy. In reality, however, most crime scenes were gruesome, with one or more dead bodies found in such ways that made you want to throw up. Rarely did you find enough evidence throughout the investigation to find the bad guy, and so eventually, most homicide cases turned cold.

On those rare occasions that the killer was caught, their lawyers would most often get them off with a plea deal. "What was the point of it anymore?" thought the Detective. He took another long drag of the cigarette before throwing it to the ground and stepping on it. "Time to go to work," he thought to himself with very little enthusiasm. As he moved beyond the police tape and entered the home, he noticed that the living room was nicely decorated. The walls had many family photos—photos of what looked like a married couple and their twin daughters—all smiling and laughing… all except one photo.

Detective Marshal moved closer to the frame to inspect the image in more detail—a man and a woman, holding hands, looking at each other lovingly. Next to them were the same twin girls as in the other pictures, but they looked different somehow. For one, the way they were dressed didn't match any of their other photos. Their clothing was much darker, and they weren't smiling, just looking oddly at the male figure. The Detective also noticed there was something about their eyes. He couldn't quite put his finger on it, but it gave him a chill.

"Detective Marshal!" he looked up from the photo to see Jenkins, a new, younger addition to the homicide unit, calling out to him from the kitchen, where he had been told the body was found. He made a mental note to look more into what was so unsettling about the picture—after all, many a case had been cracked thanks to his gut instinct—and moved into the kitchen. The kitchen was clean and well organized like the rest of the house, all except for the lifeless form of a caucasian woman lying on the floor.

"What do we have here?" he asked the medical examiner, still squatting next to the body.

"I found this ID on her," she said, handing over a laminated card to the detective, "that identifies her as Sarah Brown; 37. There are no visible wounds on the body, except," she paused as she moved toward the woman's feet, "these marks from maybe a very thin rope or a cord having been tightly wound around her ankles. I'd have to take the body back to the lab to try and pick up microfibres off the skin and tell you anything for sure."

Marshal crouched down next to the body's feet to get a closer look. There was a deep depression on her ankles as if something sharp had been used to tightly bind her feet together. There were droplets of blood here and there from where the skin had broken, but nothing had spilled out onto the ground.

"Any guess about the cause of death?" inquired the detective, seeing as there was no blood or obvious wounds.

"So far, it looks like a possible drug overdose, or maybe some form of poison. In any case, whatever killed this woman, went in the oral route. But, again, I won't know for sure until I do the autopsy. All I can tell you right now is that she's been dead for at least an hour or hour and a half."

Marshal nodded and then turned to Jenkins, "Who called it in?"

"911 received the call at around 4 pm this afternoon from the victim's daughter…" he paused to pull out a little notebook, "…Anna Brown, aged 11. The 911 records show that the girl said that her mother's boyfriend, Mr. Ron Johnson, was fighting with the girl's mother and made her take some pills. When one of our units showed up, they found Mr. Johnson in the living room passed out on the ground. Shortly after that, our unit found our victim Mrs. Brown here on the kitchen floor, already dead. Mr. Johnson was taken to the hospital by the EMT for possible drug overdose since we found empty bottles of prescription medication by both parties, and Mr. Johnson wasn't responsive."

"Doesn't the victim have two daughters? Twins?" he asked, based on the photographs he'd seen in the living room.

"Yes, both the girls were taken by the unit to Child Protective Services. They will take care of them until they can find the next of kin," replied Jenkins.

"You said it was reported that the victim's boyfriend fought with her and forced prescription drugs down her?"

"Yes, the 911 call said the young girl saw the couple fight and that the boyfriend had forced her mother to take pills."

"I see no signs of a struggle in the apartment, no knocked over furniture, and the forensic analyst confirmed that there are no bruises on the victim indicating any physical attack; how do you think that adds up?" he looked directly at Jenkins, who just shook his head in response.

"What about the marks on the ankle. Any theories?" Marshal probed more; he liked to work the younger crop to get them thinking more.

"Maybe the boyfriend bound her ankles to keep her from getting away?" Jenkins offered. "Possibly, did you or anyone else find any rope or anything that looks like it was used to bind her?" he followed.

"No sir, nothing of the like was found so far," replied Jenkins.

"Do you have anything else for me?"

"We did find an older ID for Sarah and know that her maiden name is Claymore."

"Okay, have someone canvas the area, see if the neighbors heard shouting or sounds of fighting coming from the house. I also need anything and everything you can find on the boyfriend. Send one of the uniformed guys down to the hospital; I want his statement the minute he wakes up. Keep me posted." He began walking for the door, ready to get back to his desk and deal with the pile of open cases waiting for him. Then suddenly, as if realizing something, he paused for a moment, and turning back to Jenkins, he asked. "Where did the unit find the twins when they arrived?"

"That was the weird thing. When the unit arrived, they said they had found the twin girls sitting on the living room floor right next to the boyfriend playing with their dolls as if nothing had happened."

Chapter 1
Another Day

"Cock-a-doodle-do," came the familiar morning call from a rooster outside. Earl Claymore slowly opened his eyes, allowing the sleep to fade away before getting out of bed. There was a faint light creeping in the farmhouse bedroom window as the sun began to rise on yet another beautiful morning. The smell of bacon wafted up the stairs to his nose's delight. That would be his wife Edith downstairs, already getting the day's breakfast ready for him before he started his usual routine around the farm. He slowly sat up and rubbed his aching knees to get the circulation flowing through his legs again. Every year his arthritis kept getting worse, but the doctors said there wasn't much they could do for him at his age.

Despite arthritis, he was far from a weak, frail person; in fact, he was the exact opposite. Earl was a big man, over six feet tall, and his muscles were still very strong from all the years working the farm. Even though he had a full head of pure white hair and a white stubble to match, his bright blue eyes still showed the mischief of youth. Still, he would be turning 65 this winter, and time was definitely catching up with his joints, even if he chose to deny it.

"Has it really been that long?" Earl mumbled to himself.

Farm life was consistent and mundane, which allowed time to slip by without too much notice. But, not once had he ever regretted his calling in this life. He loved being a farmer. There was always a great sense of accomplishment when working the land with your own two hands. Slipping out of bed, he put on his shirt and favorite overalls, which were now a faded blue from many years of use. After getting dressed, he went downstairs to what would be another hearty breakfast that only Edith could make.

Earl entered the kitchen and saw that Edith was cooking some eggs on the stove. He glanced over at the kitchen table and saw that it had already been loaded up with many breakfast items. There was a basket full of fresh biscuits, jam, churned butter, fresh-squeezed orange juice, smoked maple bacon, and a small porcelain creamer filled with cream for the coffee.

The kitchen itself, as was the rest of the house, was all built with hand-crafted wood from the finest oak. There were beautiful antique candlelight holders throughout the kitchen instead of modern lighting. Edith insisted she loved a candle-lit room over any other light, saying it always gave the room a romantic appeal. The candles were already blown out, for the early morning sun was shining through the large bay windows and flooding the entire kitchen with its warm light.

Earl stood there a little while looking lovingly at his wife. She was very short in stature, only topping at a little over five feet. She had long white hair that she always wore in a bun on the top of her head tied up in a blue ribbon. Her hazelnut-colored eyes were as sharp as ever, never needing glasses. She was wearing her favorite blue dress this morning; it used to be her mother's. The dress was plain and simple, but it was the last thing Edith's mother gave to her before she had passed away. She was also wearing a floral patterned apron around her robust middle. Although she was the same age as Earl himself—and a little on the plumper side—she moved with the grace of a ballerina as she navigated around the kitchen. They had been high school sweethearts and had gotten married a couple of years after they had graduated. They would be celebrating their 43rd wedding anniversary coming September. Earl knew as he stood there watching his beautiful wife go about her usual morning routine, unaware of his presence, that he loved her more now than the first day they had met.

"Yikes!" Edith screamed as Earl wrapped his large arms around her giving her a start. She turned her head quickly and looked up at him.

"Earl, stop that! You almost caused my old heart to stop!" Edith exclaimed as she playfully slapped at his arms.

"Nonsense, your heart is as strong as a horse," Earl said, smiling down at her. He then leaned down and kissed her lovingly.

"Alright, that's enough of that," Edith said after a few moments, flushing red as she pulled away from him to finish getting breakfast ready.

Earl sat down in his favorite oak chair and slid

himself forward toward the table. Edith quickly came over and sat his cup of steaming coffee down in front of him before heading back to get his food. He filled his coffee with fresh cream just the way he loved as his wife came immediately back with a plate that had two eggs sunny side up on it and a bowl of gravy which she sat down on the table in front of him. Earl then loaded his plate up with the maple bacon as Edith got her own plate and sat down at the table across from him. He grabbed a couple of biscuits from the basket, putting them on the plate. He then poured a generous amount of gravy or what folks around these parts called 'sloppins' all over the biscuits. Edith put her hands together, closed her eyes, and prayed. Edith had always been the religious type, and their house showed it with all the angel figurines, crosses, and pictures of Jesus. Earl, on the other hand, was a numbers guy. He believed when your number was up, that was it. He watched his wife pray as she had done every meal they had shared together. He didn't mind her beliefs, for if there was a God, then surely her prayers would keep them both safe.

"You know Sarah is bringing the twins down to visit this weekend," Edith said after finishing her prayer as she started to spread fresh strawberry jam onto her biscuit.

"Really?" Earl asked with obvious skepticism in his voice as he took a bite of the maple bacon.

Sarah was their daughter and the only child they ever had. Growing up, Sarah had always been a sweet loving child that had always seen the good in everything. She was very outgoing, which made her very popular in school, and very pretty, which made her very popular with all the boys—much to Earl's disliking. However, Earl never had anything really to worry about because Sarah was very strong and independent, never falling into the typical teenage traps.

Growing up, Sarah was always going around town to help out wherever she could, and the entire town loved her for it. However, as Sarah started to reach adulthood, her thirst for knowledge and excitement beyond the farm life became too much for her. So when she graduated from high school, it was natural that she immediately moved to the big city of St. Louis. That is where Sarah eventually met her future husband, Neil Brown, and fell in love. Both Earl and Edith took an immediate liking to Neil. He was a caring, loving man, and to Earl, it was important that Neil always put Sarah first and treated her like a Queen. After a couple of years together, Sarah and Neil got married and had twin girls, Anna and Anabel. Sarah had often visited Earl and Edith with her growing family to their delight. Edith especially loved the visits because she would fawn over the grandchildren and spoil them rotten, which the twins always seemed to enjoy. The twins were also much like their parents; both were sweet and always wanted to help out with things.

However, after Sarah's husband Neil died three years ago, Sarah stopped coming to visit. It was sad about Neil's death and how it happened. Sarah had come home from work one day and found the twins playing in the front yard alone. Neil was supposed to have taken the girls to school that morning. Afraid that something had happened, Sarah asked the twins where daddy was, and they had said he was in the garage. Sarah went to the garage to check on Neil, only to find his car still running and his dead body in the driver's seat behind the wheel.

The death was ruled a suicide by carbon monoxide poisoning. This came as a shock to everyone because

Neil never showed any signs of anything ever being wrong. Ever since Neil's death, Sarah would often make promises to come to visit but always found some excuse not to. Thus, Earl had his doubts she would be coming this time as well.

"The girls will be 12 years old this year. How much they must have grown by now!" Edith exclaimed excitedly as she finished her first biscuit and started on the bacon. "I miss their free spirits and laughter."

"Will Ron be coming with them?" Earl asked unenthusiastically about the prospect. Ron was Sarah's new boyfriend, a guy she met about six months ago. Earl had only met Ron once when he went up to drop some items off to Sarah that she wanted from storage. Earl immediately didn't care too much for Ron; there was something off about him. Earl couldn't quite put his finger on it, but he just knew deep down inside that Ron wasn't trustworthy.

"No," Edith replied as she picked up her second biscuit. " He has a big project coming up, and he has to finish it this weekend."

"I'll bet he does," Earl mumbled with obvious disgust on his face. Ron was a lawyer and always seemed to make excuses to spend more time at work than at home with Sarah. "That fellow isn't right, mark my words."

"Oh, come now! You stop with your nonsense Earl Claymore, or I won't bake my famous peach cobbler this weekend when the girls come! Do you hear me?!" Edith exclaimed, pointing a biscuit at him accusingly. "I know you miss Neil, we all do, God rest his poor soul, but that doesn't give you a right to judge poor Ron so harshly. Especially since you only met him one time, and he seems to be taking good care of Sarah. Besides, it's good that Sarah has finally moved on with her life."

"Alright, you win!" Earl exclaimed, smiling. "Threatening to not bake your famous peach cobbler is just cruel, though."

Edith seeing the mischievous gleam in Earl's eyes, couldn't help but join in his mirth.

***

Later that day, Earl was replacing a couple of damaged pieces of wood on the fence that surrounded his small farm when he heard a familiar oinking noise approaching from behind.

Even without looking, he knew it was Betsy, the pig. It also meant that her owner John Colt wasn't too far behind. Turning around, Earl saw he was correct because a very large pig was running excitedly at him. Behind Betsy came a tall, well-muscled young man in military pants and shirt. The man had dark red hair cut military style and eyes that had seen way too much. Earl kneeled down and gave Betsy a big hug and a playful pat on her rump as she collided with him.

"G-good afternoon Mr. Claymore," John called to Earl as he approached.

John was the closest thing to a neighbor and friend Earl had out here. He lived in a trailer on a plot of land next to Earl's that was left to him by his father when he passed away. John was an Army Ranger, or at least he used to be. He had been deployed in the Middle East when he heard of his father's passing and, later that same year, decided to come home after being in an explosion caused by enemy fire. This incident had a lasting impact on the man and had caused him some brain trauma, leaving him a bit strange.

"Good morning to you as well, John," replied Earl, getting back up to shake John's outstretched hand. "I see Betsy is doing well and loving life."

"Yes, Sir, Sh-she is very content with her station this d-day," replied John, slowly forming the words. Part of the trauma he had suffered to his head had left him with a small stutter. John leaned down and patted Betsy on her rump, which made her roll around widely on the ground. Betsy was John's best friend, and the two were inseparable except for the rare occasions John went into town.

"How about you, John?" Earl asked.

"I am d-doing well. I just got b-back from t-town this morning," John replied.

Earl noticed that every time he spoke of coming back from the town, he would always look down at the ground with slumped shoulders. John did not go into town too often, but when he did, the younger generation of town folk and some of the older folk too, apparently, would often make fun of John's condition. It wasn't right for a war hero to be treated that way, Earl thought to himself.

"Th-the new Sheriff arrived y-yesterday." John continued. "Sher-iff Bowman finally re-tired."

"Hmm, new Sheriff, you say," Earl replied, absently petting the pig that was now trying to eat his boot. "Well, Sheriff Bowman was getting a little long in the tooth. I guess it was about time."

"The new Sher-iff is a young woman from the th-the city. Her name is C-claire Davis, she is v-very pleasant to t-talk to," said John blushing, his cheeks turned red, which was highlighted by his red hair.

"I'm taking her as a pretty woman?" asked Earl, smiling. He could guess the answer and why John's cheeks were as red as his barn.

"Yes, she is a handsome w-woman indeed. We talked for a w-while this morning alone," John said with his head down and looking at his boots.

"NOOOOOOOOOOO!" came a horrible cry from the other side of the farmhouse. Earl and John stood there a moment staring at each other, not comprehending what exactly they were hearing.

"Edith," both men said, realizing it at the same time. Then John was off sprinting fast toward the farmhouse. Earl tried his best to catch up with John, but his arthritic knees wouldn't let him go very fast, and soon even

Betsy passed him.

With his breath coming in labored gasps and his legs aching painfully, Earl finally came around the side of the farmhouse to the front yard. What he saw stole what little breath he had left. There, lying on the ground, was Edith, her head on John's knee, eyes barely open. On the other side of Edith kneeled a woman Earl had never seen before. The woman was dressed in an officer's uniform and was saying something to John, who quickly got up and ran into the farmhouse. After a few moments, John came running back out with a towel and pitcher full of water. Earl, finally catching his breath, came running up to the three. As he approached, the woman officer poured water on the towel, wrung it out, and then wiped Edith's face with it while John held Edith's head in his lap again.

"Dear God! Edith, what's wrong! Are you alright?!" Earl cried out in panic. "She's dead," That was all Edith said before she passed out.

Chapter 2
A Message Delivered

Earl was sitting at the kitchen table staring vacantly into a cup of tea that John had recently set in front of him. His mind replayed the traumatic events that had just happened. He remembered coming around the farmhouse and seeing Edith's prone form just lying there on the ground. He remembered his fear at that moment that she was dead. When he found that she was alive, his fear briefly eased. But then it immediately rose again as he had heard Edith's haunting words, "she's dead," before passing out. John had then picked Edith up and brought her limp form inside the farmhouse, where he gently placed her onto the living room couch. The woman who had wiped down Edith's head with the cool, wet towel had quickly grabbed a pillow and put it under her head. John then brought a blanket and draped it over Edith. Earl remembered just standing there in the doorway, watching it all, unable to move until John quickly led him into the kitchen and sat him down.

"Mr. Claymore?" came a call that jolted Earl out of his thoughts. He looked up at where the voice had come from to see that it was the lady officer standing at the entrance to the kitchen. The woman was tall, close to six feet. She had short-cropped black hair and hazelnut eyes that looked like they had little gold flakes in them when the sunlight hit them. Her skin was flawless, and her lips were full, which created a very youthful appearance. Looking at her, Earl would place her in her late twenties. Closer inspection of her uniform showed Earl that she was the new Sheriff that John had spoken of earlier.

"Mr. Claymore?" the question came again.

"Yes, yes, I'm sorry," Earl said, trying to focus.

"Hello, Mr. Claymore. I am Sheriff Claire Davis," she moved closer as she said this and offered an outstretched hand to Earl. Earl absently shook her hand, still trying to get his thoughts and emotions under control.

"Edith?" Earl asked, finally in control.

"Your wife is resting now and will be fine," offered the Sheriff. "She just fainted and needs some rest."

John brought the Sheriff a cup of tea and pulled out a chair at the table for her to sit down in. Claire sat down, thanking John while giving him a small smile. John, blushing fiercely, quickly went back to leaning on the kitchen counter, looking down at his feet.

"I'm sorry, Mr. Claymore, but I, unfortunately, have some very unpleasant news to give you concerning your daughter, Sarah." started the Sheriff with as much compassion as she could.

"Sarah?" asked Earl. Oh dear God, what has happened to his little Sarah, Earl thought. Remembering Edith's haunting words, "she's dead," there immediately was a hollow pit in his stomach—a feeling that wanted to make him vomit.

"Mr. Claymore, I was contacted by Detective James Marshall from the St. Louis police department this morning about your daughter Sarah. Detective Marshall wanted to confirm if you and Edith were Sarah's parents…" she paused for a moment, dreading what she was about to say.

"Were?" asked Earl, his voice cracking and tears starting to form in his eyes.

"Mr. Claymore, Detective Marshall has informed me that your daughter was murdered last night by her boyfriend, Ron Johnson. I am truly sorry for your loss," replied the Sheriff.

"Dear God! No!! It can't be. There has to be some mistake!" cried Earl.

"Mr. Claymore, " began the Sheriff as she reached out for his hand to try and comfort him.

"NO! YOU'RE WRONG! YOU'RE WRONG! YOU'RE WRONG!" Earl screamed over and over, jerking his hand away from the Sheriff's and jumping out of his seat, knocking his chair clear across the floor. John was by Earl's side in an instant, holding him tightly by the shoulders, which was no easy feat. Earl tried to struggle to get free, but John's grip was like a vice, and eventually, Earl stopped struggling. He put his head on John's shoulder and began to sob uncontrollably. After some time, John slowly helped Earl back to the table and sat him down on one of the other chairs.

He waited a few moments to make sure Earl wasn't going to do anything more and then went to retrieve the chair Earl had sent across the room. Many moments passed before Earl gained somewhat control over his emotions.

"Mr. Claymore, I am truly sorry for your loss." repeated the Sheriff after seeing Earl regain some of his composure. "I recently lost someone that meant very much to me, and I know how it can mess you up inside. Even now, I still see him in my head every day."

Claire looked down at her hands and took a deep breath to steady herself. She had to get through this; she had to hold it together.

"There is something else I need to tell you. Your daughter Sarah had named Edith and you as the legal guardians of her twin daughters. Child Services will be bringing the girls here tomorrow if that's alright with you."

"Yes, yes, of course," said Earl, getting control of his emotions at hearing the mention of the twins. He knew he had to get it together for them and Edith.

"Edith?" Earl said aloud as he thought of her. "I'm sorry, but I need to be with my wife now."

"Yes, of course," said Claire as she stood up. "We will let ourselves out."

She and John made their way to the front door as Earl went into the living room and sat down by Edith. John was the first out the door, while Claire paused a moment to look at the couple. Earl gently grabbed Edith's hand in his and began to sob again. Claire slowly closed the door behind her as she left, trying not to make a sound. Once outside, Claire found John standing at the porch stairs with Betsy lying in the grass by his side.

"Thank you so much for helping get Mrs. Claymore into the house and for helping with Mr. Claymore in the kitchen. I don't think I could have handled any of it without your help," she said, honestly grateful for John's assistance. She really didn't know what she would have done if he hadn't been there.

"I w-was glad I c-could help. The Claymores m-mean a lot to me," John replied. He quickly looked down at the ground as Claire smiled at him in appreciation. Betsy looked up at him and cocked her head at an angle to study him.

"Will you stay around a while to keep an eye on them?" Claire asked, feeling her own stomach turn at her own recent loss. " It's just never easy to lose someone you love."

"Yes, I-I will stay out here for a w-while and work on t-the fence," John assured her.

"We make a good team. Maybe you should sign up to be a deputy," Claire said, trying to lighten the mood. "I think we would make a great team."

"I don't t-think that w-would be a g-good idea," John replied.

Claire noticed that John immediately looked at the ground instead of at her. His shoulders seemed to sink down as if someone had put a tremendous amount of weight on them. She didn't know what she had said to cause this kind of response. She had only meant the offer jokingly. Although, if she had only offered it jokingly, why did it sting her when John turned the offer down? She thought to herself. No matter her intentions, her offer somehow caused John some discomfort.

"I'm sorry, I didn't mean the offer for real. I mean, I really didn't want you as my Deputy. Wait, I don't mean I wouldn't want you as my Deputy; I just want you with me. Wait!..." Claire stopped and was horrified at what was coming out of her mouth. What the hell was she saying? Seeing John looking at her as if she was completely off her rocker only made her feel more uncomfortable. At that moment, all she wanted to do was sink into the ground and vanish.

"It's a-alright, I know what you h-had meant," John assured her. He liked the way being around Claire made him feel. Although he knew that Claire had only been trying to lighten the mood by the offer, it made him feel a little sad because if she had been serious, he wouldn't have been any help to her. All he was trained to do was kill. However, after seeing Claire stumble over her words just now, he couldn't resist having some fun with her. "You w-wanted me to be your personal secretary. I am h-highly offended, w-when will I b-be respected for my mind?"

Claire just stared at him speechless for a moment before comprehending that he was messing with her. She smiled at herself for acting like a fool. She leaned her head down as if she had been shamed and put her head into John's chest. All of a sudden, it was John's turn to want to sink down to the ground and vanish. Just the touch of Claire sent his anxiety through the roof.

Not knowing what to do, John just stood there blushing fiercely. Finally, Claire looked up at him and gave him a mischievous smile, then got into her police cruiser and drove away. John watched her drive away with all these different emotions running through him. Then he heard the weeping coming from inside the Claymore's house and remembered the gravity of the current situation.

***

"Cock-a-doodle-do" came the familiar morning call from the rooster outside.

Earl slowly opened his eyes, allowing the sleep to fade away before getting out of bed. There was a faint light creeping in the farmhouse bedroom window as the sun began to rise on yet another beautiful morning.

"What?" he exclaimed out loud and quickly sat up, taking a quick moment to look around the room. Smelling the bacon coming up the stairs, his heart jumped. "It was all a nightmare. Just a bad dream."

Feeling relieved, he quickly got dressed and headed down the stairs to see Edith.

However, when he entered the kitchen this time, he

didn't find his wife twirling around. Instead, he found the table set with a half attempt at breakfast and Edith sitting there staring into space. Her eyes were red, bloodshot, and still wet with tears. It hadn't been a bad dream, after all, and suddenly Earl's heart sank. It was true; his little girl Sarah was truly gone from this world.

"Edith," Earl called quietly.

She turned around with a start at the sound of his voice. Seeing him standing there looking at her, she jumped up and went to grab his coffee. Swiftly, as if to hide it from her husband, she ran a hand across her cheeks to wipe the tears off her wet cheeks, but Earl still saw it. It broke his heart even more. He grieved Sarah for himself, but in this moment where his wife was trying to seem strong, he grieved for her too. She turned around with resolve plastered on her face, which wasn't doing the best job of hiding the pain behind it, and addressed him.

"Hurry up and eat your breakfast. We have to get ready for the girls. They should be arriving here shortly. My dear, this house is a mess; we must get it scrubbed and cleaned." As she poured his coffee, she added, "So much to do and such a short time to do it."

He wanted to reach out his hand and hold hers, but she quickly turned around and walked to the counter to return the coffee pot. He could see the tremble in her body that she wasn't acknowledging when suddenly the pot slipped out of her grasp. With a loud crash, the glass pot shattered into small fragments that went flying across the floor.

"Dear God! Look what I have done, how careless of me!" Edith exclaimed in horror. "I have to get this picked up before the girls come and get hurt!" She immediately got down on her knees and started picking up sharp pieces of glass with her bare hands. The very next second, Earl saw her jerk one of her hands to her side. She had cut herself on one of the glass shards. Stifling a cry out loud, she began to sob uncontrollably. He quickly walked up to her and helped her up, leading her back to the chair, where he sat her gently down.

"Everything is going to be alright," Earl whispered into her ear. "We will be there for the twins, and we will all get through this together, as a family."

"How? How are we going to raise two girls at our age? How can we continue without Sarah, my baby Sarah?" Edith sobbed into Earl's shoulder.

"Look, I don't have all the answers right now, but I just know we have to do it for Sarah," Earl said as he held Edith tightly against him. "Besides, you were a great mother to Sarah, and look at how well she grew up. Also, remember every time the twins came to visit, they were always so eager to help out with things, just like Sarah did when she was young? I am sure they are exactly the same now as they were then. Heck, they probably will be the ones taking care of us instead of the other way around."

"You're absolutely right!" exclaimed Edith. She had been a good mother to Sarah and raised her right. The twins were so much like their mother that they would be great to have around. Quickly jumping out of Earl's arms, Edith grabbed the broom and gave it to Earl.

"What am I supposed to do with this?" Earl asked, not understanding the sudden change in Edith.

"It is for you to clean up the mess and when you're done with that, hurry upstairs to get dressed," Edith replied as she briskly left the kitchen.

"What about breakfast?" Earl shouted, but it was too late. Edith was already gone. Earl looked at the mess on the ground and then at the table with his breakfast. Sighing, he started to sweep up the broken glass.

***

Hours later, around midday, a green station wagon came driving up the gravel road to the front of the Claymore's home. Earl and Edith, hearing the vehicle approach, immediately came out to greet the visitors. Both Edith and Earl were dressed in their Sunday best at Edith's request, even though Earl felt it was really more of a demand. But, not wanting to upset her, he put on his best suit, which really was his only suit. The couple met the vehicle as it came to a stop in front of the house. The car door opened, and a short elderly woman got out of the car.

She was on the plump side, and the way she was dressed gave one the impression of an old school teacher. The old lady approached the Claymores to shake their hands, almost falling a few times because she was trying to walk on the gravel path with high heels on.

"Greetings, Mr. and Mrs. Claymore!" exclaimed the lady, "What a pleasure to meet the both of you. My name is Susan Wiles."

"Hello, I am Earl Claymore, and this here is my lovely wife Edith," Earl greeted as he shook Mrs. Wile's hand. "I believe you are the one Edith had spoken to on the phone."

"Yes, indeed," replied Mrs. Wiles.

"Where are they? Where are the girls?" Edith exclaimed, too nervous and excited to continue with formalities.

"Ah yes, I had them wait in the car to give you folks a moment. Please let me get them for you," answered Mrs. Wiles.

She then stumbled her way back to the car and opened the back door. The twins came out of the car, each with a doll in their hands. With their heads down, they slowly approached their grandparents. Edith impatiently ran to them and grabbed both girls into a tight embrace, telling both girls repeatedly that everything was going to be alright now that they were there. Earl noticed that the girls did not return the embrace; instead, they both just calmly stared at Mrs. Wiles as if no one else was there. They must still be in shock, Earl thought, poor things.

The girls definitely looked as if they had been mourning. They both had dark circles under their eyes, and although they had grown a lot since the last time he saw them, they were on the thin side, almost as if they were malnourished. Well, it's nothing Edith's cooking can't fix. Yep, they will be back to healthy little girls in no time, he thought.

"Who do you young ladies have with you here?" Edith asked the girls as she let the twins out of her embrace and indicated at the dolls each of them had. "What are their names?"

"Lisa and Lucy," replied Anna and Anabel in quiet tones while not taking their eyes off Mrs. Wiles.

"Well, the girls are now in your custody, so I will be leaving you, folks, now." Mrs. Wiles said, breaking the silence while also staring back at the girls oddly. She then turned and hurriedly started back to her car.

"What about the paperwork," called out Earl.

"I will send it over to you. I must be going now," Mrs. Wiles said as she quickly started to get into the vehicle.

"Bye, Susan," said the twins at the same time in even tones.

Earl noticed Mrs. Wiles gave a start, and she looked back at the girls strangely, then got into her car without another word. Soon Mrs. Wiles was driving away from the house, and Edith took the girls inside, promising both of them some peach cobbler. Earl stood there a while watching the vehicle vanish down the road, wondering what that was all about.

***

Later that evening, Earl came into the kitchen as Edith made final touches to the dinner.

Earl noticed that she had made some of the dishes that Sarah had loved growing up and must have figured that Sarah had cooked some of them for the girls at some point. The table was loaded with cornish game hens, fried pork cutlets, mashed potatoes (covered in sloppins, of course), corn on the cob, cranberry sauce, sweet potato pie, and of course, peach cobbler. The table was covered with an array of dishes, and in the center sat a centerpiece filled with a bouquet of flowers from Edith's very own special flower garden. Edith really had gone all out for the girls.

"Anna, Anabel, please come into the kitchen; it's time for dinner!" Edith called out loudly as she arranged the finishing touches to the table.

The girls came into the kitchen holding their dolls and sat down without saying a word. Despite Edith fawning all over the girls all day, the twins were still very quiet, only answering with the most basic replies.

"Quickly now, everyone holds hands, so we can say Grace," said Edith as she eagerly took hold of Anabel's hand.

Earl reached out and grabbed Anna's hand, who in turn grabbed her sister's. Earl gave a quick start when he grabbed Anna's hand because it was ice cold. Thinking the coldness had to do with being malnourished, Earl gripped Anna's hand a little tighter to help heat it up. If Anna noticed his reactions to her touch, she gave no outward sign. As Edith started the prayers, Earl took that time to study the twins more closely.

They were identical, so much so that Earl never could tell which one was which. Sarah never helped the matter by always dressing them in the same clothes and having them with the same hairstyle. Even now, sitting there, both girls were wearing identical dresses. The dresses were black and plain, nothing like the flowered dresses they had worn when they were younger. Both of them had their hair long in the back and cut just above their eyes in the front. Their hair was black, which only highlighted their pale complexion more, and in the candle-lit room, it gave them both a haunting look. How much the both of them had changed since the last time they had come down with Sarah and Neil, thought Earl to himself.

"Amen!" as Edith finished the prayer, it pulled Earl out of his head. He found himself quickly pulling his hand away from Anna's and feeling relieved once the cold little hand was out of his. Even though both girls' heads were still down, he thought he saw Anna briefly smirk when he had let go of her hand.

"Isn't it so great to have the girls with us for dinner finally, Earl?" Edith asked as she started putting food on everyone's plate.

"Huh? What?" asked Earl, barely listening, still staring at Anna, for he was still trying to determine what he saw really happened or if he had just imagined it.

"I said, isn't it great the girls are finally here?" Edith repeated herself, sitting back down to her own plate now.

"Yes, yes," replied Earl as he brushed what he thought he had seen off as his imagination getting the better of him and dug into his delicious-looking dinner.

Both girls put their dolls on the table and started eating their dinner with little enthusiasm. The dolls were identical, except Anna's looked like it had seen better days. One of the eyes was missing, and one of the arms was obviously sewn back on with what looked like a fishing line.

"Girls, please remove Lisa and Lucy from the table while you eat. It's not proper dining etiquette," Edith said, smiling at the girls.

"No," replied Anna, not lifting her eyes from her dinner plate.

Edith sat there stunned for a monument trying to comprehend what she had heard. She looked at both girls still with their heads down, not sure what just happened.

"Girls, I asked you to please remove your dolls

from the dinner table so we can eat," Edith stated again, pretending she did not hear Anna's reply. "We must have a proper dinner etiquette in the eyes of our Lord."

"No." both girls said in unison.

Edith was again stunned by the reply but quickly regained her composure. She got up and started to reach for the dolls herself to remove them from the table. However, she abruptly stopped with her hands outstretched because both the girls, at that moment, slowly turned their heads and stared directly at her. In the candlelight, their ghostly pale faces and their steady stare gave Edith a shock.

"If you touch Lisa or Lucy, you will be punished like mommy and daddy," both girls said in unison.

Edith fell back into her chair, mouth wide open, but no sound came out. Earl felt a sudden chill run down his spine but quickly recovered.

"That's enough. Both of you will apologize to your grandmother, then go to your room without dinner and think about your behavior this evening," Earl scolded them.

"We are sorry, Grandma," they apologized, then

grabbed their dolls and proceeded to leave the room. As they passed by Edith, Earl thought he saw that smirk again, but this time from both of them.

After the girls were out of the room, Edith stared at her husband as if questioning what had just happened.

"They are just going through a phase after losing their parents. It will pass, and they will be back to normal. We just have to give them time." Earl assured Edith and started eating his dinner. Edith looked at him with uncertainty but followed suit and began eating after a few moments. They both ate in silence, lost in their own thoughts.

Chapter 3
The Funeral

A week passed without any more problems from the girls. Although both were still very silent most of the time, they did behave themselves with proper manners. Edith chalked up their previous behavior to a way of grieving the loss of their mother, just like Earl had said. Earl, on the other hand, was still disturbed by the girls' behavior that night. He could not get the eerie way the girls looked in the candlelight out of his head. There was also the matter of the smirks he knew he had seen. Not to mention the creepy chill he had gotten when he grabbed Anna's hand. Even now, thinking about it sent a cold shiver running down his spine, causing his body to give a quick shake. Stop it! He scolded himself, it was simply the girls acting out for attention, and that was all it was.

"Sorry for your loss," offered Mrs. Baker, a short and stout old woman with very thick eyeglasses. Glad to have his mind brought back to the present from his less than pleasant thoughts, Earl thanked Mrs. Baker.

Earl and Edith had been standing here inside Devon Funeral Home for over an hour. All the town folks who had known Sarah growing up had been coming up to the two of them to tell them how sorry they were for their loss. Earl still had a hard time coming to terms with what was happening. Here they were greeting people as if they were at some kind of award ceremony, while across the room from them was the casket that held their beloved little girl. He couldn't believe that although he was in the same room as his daughter, he wouldn't be able to hear her laugh—not today, not ever again. When they had first brought the casket into the viewing room, he had walked over and looked in. She was lying there in a beautiful white dress with her hair styled just the way she had liked it. There were many times while she was growing up when he and Edith would just watch her sleep. It was very similar to that, except this time, he knew she wouldn't join them at the breakfast table the next morning.

Earl remembered thinking that Sarah looked so peaceful, as if she was just taking a much-needed rest. But she wasn't resting. She was dead; murdered by that bastard Ron Johnson! Choking back the lump that was starting to form in his throat Earl thanked another group of people who had just given their condolences.

***

Claire sat in her car outside the funeral home, trying to muster up enough courage to go inside. She really didn't even know what she was doing here since she didn't know Sarah or even the Claymores, for that matter. In fact, Claire didn't really know anyone in town. She had only been Sheriff for a few weeks. The only people she had really spoken to and gotten to know somewhat were her deputy Travis Jones and Sallie Mae, the dispatcher. Also, of course, there was John Colt, who had been coming into town more and more lately. So why was she here? *I'm here because I had told a sweet old couple that their daughter was murdered by some drugged-up asshole, and I feel that I now need to do something for them,* Claire thought to herself.

Claire grew up in St. Louis, and the injustices she saw there, combined with the city's growing homicide rate, made her vow to become a cop. So as soon as she had graduated high school, she immediately went to the police academy to make a change. She graduated at the top of her class and became a police officer earlier than expected. Claire quickly earned her way up the ladder by aiding in the capture of a serial killer, for which she won a medal. This recognition got her a promotion to become a detective, a position she had always wanted, or so she had thought. She had become a cop to stop people like Sarah from getting murdered. However, a week before her promotion was to take place, her partner at the time, Dan Lowe, was shot and killed while they were answering a domestic abuse call. She and Dan had gotten very close during their partnership, closer perhaps than they should have. They had tried to keep their relationship professional, but she and Dan just couldn't seem to help themselves. They had even planned to get married after she became Detective. Yet, when they had shown up to the abuse call, the suspect in question shot Dan in the head right in front of Claire. Without thinking, Claire emptied her entire mag into the perp's chest. She had both lost and taken a life that night, which in turn had destroyed a part of her. Even though the judge had ruled that she had acted rightfully in self-defense, she was no longer eligible for the Detective promotion. Claire had felt it was for the best anyway, for she felt she couldn't stay with the department after Dan's death. She still wanted to be a cop, but somewhere far away from there. So, when she had heard from a friend that there was a sheriff's position opening up in a small town outside the city, she decided to take it. She figured that the biggest crime out there would be to find out who had been tipping cows. How dangerous could it be, she had thought to herself. Yet, here she was about to give condolences to the Claymores and pay respects to yet another life taken through a senseless murder.

"C-Claire?" The question that came outside her car window startled Claire.

"Sweet Jesus!" screamed Claire jumping in her seat. She turned and saw it was just John standing there. She immediately grabbed her chest to keep her pounding heart from flying out.

"Dammit, John! You scared the hell out of me!" Claire scolded him in between labored breaths.

"Sss-sorry," John apologized, obviously ashamed for causing Claire distress. "I didn't me-mean to sc-scare you."

"No, it's alright, John. I didn't mean to yell at you like that," Claire apologized, calming down at seeing how hurt John had gotten by her comment. After all, it wasn't John's fault that her mind went off to Never Neverland. "It's alright, really. I was just lost in thought."

John opened the car door for Claire, and she reluctantly got out. She stood there for a moment, looking at the funeral home, again imagining her partner's dead body on the ground. She unknowingly reached out and grabbed John's hand. Lost in thought, Claire didn't see John's face turn scarlet red at her touch. She came out of her thoughts a moment later at John's gentle squeeze of her hand and looked up at him. Claire saw on John's face that he somehow knew what she was feeling. This didn't surprise her because she knew John had been in the military. She knew that he had been in an explosion where he had lost a lot of his brothers, so it only made sense that he would understand death and loss intimately. For some reason, John's understanding made Claire more at ease. Giving him a small smile of gratitude, Claire turned toward the funeral home. Still holding John's hand, they went inside together.

Upon entering the funeral home, Claire saw quite a few of the town folk she had briefly met before since taking her new role as the Sheriff. They were all dressed in black, quietly talking among one another in small groups. A short way in from the entrance of the funeral parlor, on the right-hand side along the wall, stood Mr. and Mrs. Claymore. The couple was approached by yet another group of people wanting to give their condolences to them. Suddenly, Claire started to feel pain in her hand, the hand John was holding. Looking down, she saw that John had tightened his grip so much that his knuckles were turning white. She looked up at John's face and saw the sheer panic in his eyes. At first, she didn't understand what was happening. Why did he look like deer caught in a headlight? John had always been a little awkward every time he and Claire were together. However, she knew that some of that awkwardness on those previous occasions they were together was due to him having feelings for her. John never said anything to Claire about his feelings, but she was a cop that was good at reading things. Like how he looked at her when he didn't think she was looking. She had to admit to herself that she liked the way he looked at her.

However, even though that awkwardness was both understandable and flattering, the look on his face now was one of sheer terror. Suddenly, the realization hit her. The times she had spoken with John previously, they had always been alone. Now, here they were, in a room with a lot of the town's folk, some of them whom Claire had heard rumors about. Rumors that mentioned some of these people would often make fun of John's disability whenever he came into town. She had also heard that there was a town bully that would always try to fight John on those occasions. This time it was Claire's turn to give John's hand a gentle squeeze. She saw him look down at her, his face and body visibly relaxing. Feeling comforted by each other's presence, the two of them made their way over to where Mr. and Mrs. Claymore stood.

"Hello, Mr. and Mrs. Claymore," began Claire, but then she suddenly stopped, trying to find the right words. "I'm sorry, I honestly don't know the right thing to say. I am just so sorry."

"It's alright, dear. Thank you so much for coming," replied Edith as she gave Claire a hug. "Thanks for coming, John," Mr. Claymore said, firmly shaking

John's hand. "Thank both you for coming and for taking care of Edith last week."

"A-any t-time. If you ev-er n-need anything, please let me know," stammered John with genuine concern.

"Will do, sweetie. You are such a good boy, John," said Edith reaching up as she tried to give John a kiss on the cheek. Even with Edith on her tippy toes, John had to bend nearly in half just to let Edith kiss him. It would have been quite comical if it hadn't been under such sorrowful circumstances, Claire thought.

"I'm so glad you and John came together. You both make a lovely couple," Edith said as she stepped back to observe the two of them approvingly.

Claire was so stunned by the comment that she couldn't speak. She knew her mouth was open, but nothing came out. She quickly glanced at poor John and saw him go white as a ghost as if someone had drained every drop of blood out of him.

"We are not together. I mean, we didn't come together. I mean, we came in together, but we didn't come together. Wait, I mean, we just met. Well, we didn't just meet… we obviously met before. Oh God, why can't I stop talking?!" Claire rambled, horrified.

"Please stop," said Mr. Claymore as he burst into a deep, hearty laugh. Mrs. Claymore soon joined her husband with her own giggles. "Edith didn't mean anything by it. She just meant that you both compliment one another very well. Thank both of you for being here for us and for giving us a little joy this day."

Claire didn't know what the hell had happened, but she was glad she had finally stopped talking. Although, John's frozen expression of humiliation made her think her incoherent speech was the least of her worries.

**

A little while later, both Claire and John were able to break away from the Claymores to regain their much-needed composure. They both were now waiting in line for their turn to pay their respects to Sarah. They were no longer holding hands, and both of them were much too embarrassed to say anything.

"I'm sorry, John, I was caught off guard back there and didn't know what I was saying," Claire apologized, finally breaking the unbearable silence.

"It's al-alright, I kn-know your n-not in-terested in

someone th-that's d-damaged," John stammered with obvious pain in his voice and his eyes to the ground.

"It's not that, really. I just don't know what I am feeling or doing about anything. I just recently lost my partner, and now all this with the Claymores. It's just becoming all too much for me right now," Claire said. She gently grabbed his hand again and gave him a small smile, which of course, caused John to turn beet-red again. She knew she had only known John for a couple of weeks, and everything was moving too fast, but there was something about John that just made her feel safe. The line kept moving until finally, it was their turn, and they proceeded to the casket to pay their respects. Both Claire and John stood there silently, both not sure what to say, yet both taking comfort from the other being there. Claire took this time to notice how peaceful Sarah seemed. The dress Sarah was being buried in was beautiful and was of the purest white. The dress ended about mid-calf leaving the ankles exposed. Just then, something on Sarah's ankle caught Claire's eye. She could make out the slightest discoloration where the makeup must have been accidentally rubbed off. It looked like the makeup was put there to cover up a bruise, and there seemed to be something else, but she couldn't quite make it out. Quickly looking around to make sure no one was watching, Claire reached into the casket and rubbed some of the makeup away, exposing what looked like a bruise with a fine line cut or scratch across the ankle.

"John, what do you make of this?" Claire whispered to John, showing him the marks on the ankle. She immediately felt John's grip tighten on her other hand. She looked up at him and saw his face was very grim. "What's wrong? Have you seen this before?"

John nodded to Claire but didn't say anything right away. He bent down and took a closer look as if to confirm what he already knew, and then he nodded to her again.

"W-war. Tr-trip wire," John stuttered, still with a grim look on his face.

"Tripwire? Detective Marshall said that Sarah died of a drug overdose, but there was no mention of her being tortured. My God, what did that sick bastard Ron Johnson do to her?" exclaimed Claire in horrified disgust.

Claire turned to leave when she noticed the Brown

twins a little way off to the side, watching her. Both girls were standing by themselves with their dolls in hand. They were wearing black dresses, and their pale skin gave her the impression of a specter. Then one of the twins brought her doll up to her ear. Claire saw her tilt her head as if she was listening to the doll tell her a secret; they both then nodded their heads in unison.

"R-ready to go?" asked John, joining Claire.

She turned to look at John, then looked back at the twins, but they were now gone. Getting a chill, she felt it was time to go.

"Yes, let's go," Claire said, still looking for the twins, but they were nowhere to be seen.

After Claire and John had left the funeral, John walked her to her car and offered to follow her home to make sure she would arrive safely. Claire suddenly started laughing at the offer, which in turn earned a confused look from John.

"I'm the Sheriff, remember? It's my job to serve and protect all of you, not the other way around," Claire said, still laughing.

John realized the thought that the Sheriff needed

protecting was kind of funny and soon joined Claire in the mirth. But soon, the laughter was gone, and then there was only uncomfortable silence. Neither one of them really wanted to part with each other's company, but they also didn't know what else to say. Claire couldn't explain it, but she just felt something or someone was watching her and somehow, John being close to her made her feel safe.

"Well, I had better be going. It's getting late, and I have to work early," Claire said, finally breaking the silence.

"L-let me get your door." John offered and nearly bowled Claire over, trying to get to the car door handle before her. He then opened the door and stepped back to let her get in. As Claire moved around the car, she paused a moment and looked at John. They were so close she could feel the heat coming from him, or maybe it was from her. Claire really didn't know which, but she did know that her heart was racing. John just gave her a sort of stiff, awkward smile. Not knowing what else to do, Claire gave an awkward smile in return and got into her car. As John gently closed the car door, Claire sat there with a feeling of disappointment. What did she expect, for him to kiss her? She didn't know what she had expected or what she was feeling, but it was too late now. Starting her car, Claire looked briefly into her rearview mirror and thought she saw the twins standing in the doorway of the funeral parlor watching her. However, when she looked again, there was no one there. Feeling that eerie feeling again, Claire felt it was definitely time to go home.

She pulled into her driveway a short time later. She saw in her side mirror a vehicle pass by, and when she looked out her car window, she saw John's truck drive away. He had followed her home anyway just to make sure she was safe. Claire slept well that night with the thoughts of seeing John again soon.

Chapter 4
What the Heart Wants

Earl and Edith sat in their rocking chairs on their front porch, contently watching the day settle into the evening. The sun was just above the horizon, getting ready to set, turning the sky into a myriad of colors. A fresh pitcher of sun-brewed iced tea sat on the table between them, along with two mason jars filled to the brim with the golden liquid. The twins were playing in the front yard with their dolls. Earl looked at the twins and thought how they had been very well-behaved since Sarah's funeral over a month ago. The girls still didn't speak a whole lot, and despite Edith's delicious meals, the girls still seemed to stay on the thin side. But, at least there were no more problems with their manners at the dinner table. In fact, they would often help clean up. The only time Earl had to scold the two of them was when he had caught them in his shed in the backyard. Aside from that, the girls were being very proper, if still a little distant. The twins still seemed to mostly prefer each other's company and, of course, their dolls.

Nonetheless, their improved behavior had brought the full grandmother out of Edith so much that she would often spend the whole day fawning over them, whether the girls liked it or not. Earl was happy to see this because the girls kept Edith's attention on them and not on the loss of their daughter Sarah. Earl felt that Edith would have handled Sarah's death very badly if it had not been for the twins being there. So watching Edith sitting there on the porch content while watching the girls play made Earl feel like life on the farm seemed to have returned somewhat back to normal. At least as normal as it could be.

"You know, I think I will take the girls to my secret spot tomorrow. I think they will love it," said Edith smiling.

"I think that would be a wonderful idea. In fact, I am surprised you haven't already shown them," responded Earl.

Ear smiled to himself as he thought of Edith's 'secret spot'—something he had built at the end of their property on the edge of the woods. Earl had found the little clearing on one of the hikes he used to take when his knees were still good. Having seen how well the soil was there and how the clearing received a great deal of sunlight, he knew it would make a perfect flower garden for Edith. He spent a long time planting all of Edith's favorite flowers and setting up a gazebo for her so she would have a place to sit to enjoy the scenery. When their 20th anniversary came around, Earl led Edith blindfolded to the clearing, and once they had arrived at the garden, Earl took off Edith's blindfold. Seeing her face as she gazed upon the garden, he knew he had done right. Tears had flown freely down both of Edith's cheeks, and her entire body had begun to shake uncontrollably. Earl remembered how after a few intense moments, Edith had turned to him and buried her face deep into his chest. They both had stayed that way, him holding her tightly in his big arms and her sobbing in his chest for what seemed like hours. It was well after dusk by the time they finally broke apart and made their way back home. Since that day, the garden had become Edith's secret spot where she often went to have time by herself.

The spot was so special to Edith that she considered it to be her Eden, and she had never taken anyone to the garden, not even Sarah.

"Looks like we have some company coming," Edith said.

Hearing Edith's voice brought Earl's attention back to the present. He looked down the driveway to see the dust cloud of a vehicle slowly approaching. Soon Earl could see that it was John's beat-up blue pickup truck coming up the drive. The truck finally came to a stop a little ways from the porch. John jumped out of the truck, then briefly leaned back in and a moment later brought out Besty putting her on the ground. Betsy immediately started rolling around in the grass. Out of the passenger side of the truck came Claire, to a not-so-surprised Earl. He knew that John had been going into town a lot the last month since the funeral to see the Sheriff. Even though going into town was always hard for John, Earl knew that John and the Sheriff were getting close. As if to prove Earl's point, Claire was not wearing her uniform; instead, she was dressed up in a simple pair of jeans and a St. Louis Cardinals t-shirt. This casual attire just showed that she was spending her off-duty time with John. As Claire came around the truck, John took her hand, and all three of the visitors approached the farmhouse.

"Good evening, John. Sheriff." greeted Earl. Betsy, the pig, came running up and started jumping on Earl's legs. Laughing, Earl reached down and roughly patted Besty on her rump. Earl swore that Besty was more human than a pig, for she was non-stop loving and constantly demanded attention. "Good evening to you as well, Betsy!"

"Good evening, Mr. and Mrs. Claymore. Please call me Claire," Claire greeted back.

"Well, if we're going to call you Claire, then we insist on you calling us Earl and Edith," said Earl warmly.

"Besides, John is family to us, and it seems that you both are finally together, which makes you family as well," said Edith with a knowing smile. Both John and Claire's faces immediately turned scarlet, and they both instinctively looked at the ground like children who had been caught doing something wrong.

"Stop that! You both don't need to be embarrassed about anything." scolded Edith in her most stern motherly voice. "As I told you both that day at the funeral, you both compliment each other well."

"Yes, well, it's just kinda happening so fast," replied Claire shyly, still not raising her head.

It was true, Claire and John's relationship had accelerated after that night at Sarah's funeral. John had shown up the very next day at the station to take Claire to lunch. He had taken her to a beautiful picnic spot just outside of town. At first, there had been the typical awkwardness of when "boy meets girl." But, as they talked and spent more time together, their conversations became more fun and exciting. They had lunch every day together for a month, and neither got bored with one other. Still, a month wasn't a very long time, and they hadn't ever really gone on a real date. Today would be their first time spending the whole day together; no pressure there, Claire thought to herself.

"Listen, the heart wants what the heart wants. It's that simple. Life is a journey filled with many roads, some good and some bad. Some roads will take longer than others, and some will arrive quicker, but they will all lead somewhere eventually. The most important thing to remember is that the good Lord gave us a heart so it could help guide us on the paths we choose. Sooner or later, that heart will lead you to the path of your one true love. You will know it's right when you look into each other's eyes, for the eyes are the gateway to one's soul," said Edith with compassion and understanding evident in her voice.

A sudden thought came to Claire, who then raised her head and looked John in the eyes. They both stared deeply at each other, and there was no mistake that what the both of them were seeing right then was each other's souls. John leaned down to Claire's lips, and she started to meet his.

"Ahem," Earl purposely cleared his throat. Not really wanting to ruin the moment, but knowing this moment was better to be had in another time and place. Both John and Claire turned to look at Earl, the moment broken. Earl noticed that this time though, that when the two of them turned toward him, they did so with their heads held high. Smiling on the inside, Earl marveled at how well Edith was with words when it came to love. "So, what do we owe the pleasure of your company this evening? Surely it wasn't loving advice from a couple of stubborn old people?"

"Who are you calling old and stubborn," Edith humphed, acting offended.

"Actually, I plan on taking Claire to the fishing cabin tonight and going fishing in the morning. I need to borrow a rod, if I can?" asked John.

Both Earl and Edith nearly fell out of their rocking chairs in disbelief. John had said the sentence perfectly without any stuttering. They both looked first at John, then at Claire, then at each other. Both shrugging, they looked back at Claire and John for an explanation.

"John has been doing well with his speech lately. I have been helping him," said Claire with a smile and looked at John warmly.

"Well, I'll be damned," said Earl, smiling now.

"Love heals all things," piped in Edith, who had a wide grin on her face.

"The r-rods, please?" asked John, obviously embarrassed by the attention.

"Yes, of course, they are in the shed outback. Come help me get them, John, and leave the womenfolk to their musings," replied Earl as he gently moved Besty off his feet and got up from the rocking chair. Earl and John then started heading toward the shed. Earl, however, couldn't resist a call out over his shoulder at the women, "You ladies behave yourselves while we are gone."

"No promises," replied both Claire and Edith at the same time, which caused both of them to burst into uncontrollable laughter.

"Well, that definitely isn't a good sign," mumbled Earl. John just nodded his head in agreement.

***

Earl and John walked around the house and approached what Earl considered a 'shed,' which was really a large storage barn that was bigger than John's entire trailer.

"So, I see you and Claire are getting along well," commented Earl as they entered the shed and made their way to the cabinet that held all of Earl's fishing and hunting gear.

"Yes, Claire has been very nice to me, and I am l-lucky to have met her," replied John. "I am just not s-s-sure I am good enough for her, though. I mean, I am nothing but a d-d-damaged killer. What could I hope to offer her?"

Earl stopped suddenly and spun to face John coming an inch from his face. He almost punched John right then, and it took everything in him not to do so. John must have sensed it because Earl noticed John take a defensive step back. Earl took a moment to calm himself and softened his expression. He loved John like a son and had always treated him as such since the first time they had met. But the thing that infuriated Earl the most was the way John viewed himself. He had grown up in an abusive family and had joined the military at the age of 18. Yes, he did become a killer. It was the typical stereotypical story. However, Earl knew that the man who stood before him was a very kind and loving person who had never been shown true love.

"Listen, John. I know all about your past, or at least what you have told me. But, do you honestly believe Edith and I would let a damaged, heartless killer into our home, into our family? We accepted you into our family, and I have always seen you as my son regardless of the different blood running through our veins. That young lady back there obviously sees the same thing in you that Edith and I do. Do you honestly believe she sees you as a damaged killer? It is you and only you who sees you as some kind of monster. It is you and only you who can change that. Just as it is you and only you who can cause you to lose something really great like true love because of something that you have imagined you are." said Earl. After a moment, Earl could see that his words had hit home, for John looked both ashamed and touched at the same time.

"Th-thank you. Thank you for everything. I promise to be the man that y-you see me as," replied John, deeply grateful for the caring words. Both men stared at each other a few moments longer and then immediately started looking everywhere except at each other. The moment had gotten extremely awkward.

"Come now, what are we women? Let's get you that fishing gear," Earl said jokingly. He then led John to the large cabinet, where he always kept fishing rods. Earl paused, noticing that the cabinet door was hanging slightly ajar. Frowning, he could have sworn he had closed it the last time he was in here.

"What's wrong?" John asked, having noticed Earl's pause and frown.

"Nothing, it's just that I thought I had closed the cabinet door the last time I was here. Must be getting old, starting to forget things," he replied with a small chuckle. Then shaking the thought off, he opened the cabinet fully. It was loaded with all kinds of camping, hunting, and fishing gear. Earl grabbed a rod and reel off a shelf and handed it to John. Then grabbed a rod from one of the shelves and put it off to the side. He then pulled out his tackle box and put it on the floor so he could open it up. Finally, he reached in and started looking for the extra roll of fishing line he had stored in there.

"Where is it? I know I put a roll of fishing line in here," Earl mumbled to himself.

"Here, let me h-help," John offered. Earl stepped back, and John looked all through the tackle box. "Not here, Maybe it's on one of the other shelves."

Both men tore through the cabinet and searched every shelf, but there was no sign of the spool of fishing line anywhere. It just didn't make any sense to Earl; he knew he had a whole roll of the fishing line and that he had put it in his tackle box the last time he went fishing.

Where could it have gone? Earl thought to himself.

"I'm sorry, John, I honestly thought I put it in my tackle box," he finally said apologetically. He knew this was a big event for John and did not want to ruin it for him.

"It's alright. I really only needed the extra r-rod. You have done enough for me this day, more than I could ever ask for," John said with sincere gratitude.

He helped Earl put everything back into the cabinet and closed the door. After grabbing the rod Earl had set aside, both men left the shed and headed back to the main house.

***

Claire couldn't remember the last time she had felt so at ease. Sitting there on the porch, chatting it up with Edith, just made everything feel right. Her emotions had been all over the place for several months. With the death of her partner Dan, the move, Sarah's funeral, and now her fast-moving relationship with John, she really hadn't had time to take a breath. However, after listening to Edith's words about roads and hearts, she started to feel more relaxed. When she had looked into John's eyes earlier, she knew that she was finally home.

"Grandma, we want some tea," stated Anna flatly as she and her sister approached the porch with their dolls in hand.

"Girls, where are our manners? How do we ask for something if we want it?" Edith asked chidingly.

"Grandma, may we please have some tea?" asked Anna again, this time properly.

Claire noticed, however, that even though she had rephrased the way she asked for the tea, her demeanor and tone were still the same. Claire also noticed that both girls' eyes seemed to have actually narrowed a little when the first one had spoken. *I wonder what that's all about*, thought Claire to herself.

"That's much better. We must always remember to show politeness to each other as our Lord has asked of us," responded Edith. If Edith had noticed the twin's eyes narrow, she didn't show it. She just smiled, obviously pleased that the girls had asked politely. "I will get you your tea, but first, I want you to meet our guest, Claire. Claire, this is Anna and Anabel."

"Hello, it's a pleasure to meet you both," Claire said with a genuine smile. "Hello." replied both girls, almost sounding robotic to Claire.

"Great! Now that introductions are out of the way, I

will go get the glasses for your tea, and you both can keep our guest entertained."

Edith then rose from her rocking chair and headed inside the house. Claire turned her attention to the twins, who were now just staring at her, not saying a word. Claire had never met the twins in person before today. But, she did remember them both from the funeral talking to their dolls and watching her. Not to mention she could have sworn she had seen them in her rearview mirror. Just then, that eerie feeling from that night came back to her.

Especially with the way the both of them were just standing there motionless, staring at her right at this moment. Claire studied both of them. They were definitely identical; no mistake about it. Both of their facial features were mirror images of each other. They also were of the same height and build. Their hair was long in the back and cut just above the eyes. Their skin was very pale, which one would not expect of children who lived on a farm and played outside a lot. Maybe they stayed inside most of the time, Claire thought to herself. They were originally suburban children, after all. But, It wasn't just the way they looked or dressed.

No, it was more than that. They both held themselves the exact same way. Also, both of their eyes were pure black, as if there were no iris, just the pupil. To add to the creep factor, both girls were wearing the exact same dresses from the funeral. As Claire stared at the both of them, she suddenly felt an odd chill run through her entire body, and she began to shake. Both girls smiled.

Claire nearly jumped out of her chair at the sound of the porch door creaking open. Edith came out with two glasses in her hands. She then grabbed the pitcher of iced tea and poured the golden nectar into both glasses. Edith then handed one glass to each of the twins. The entire time she did this, neither girl took their eyes off of Claire. Claire shifted uncomfortably. Their smiles grew.

"Girls, what do we say?" Edith asked.

"Thank you," both girls said in unison. Both of them were still staring at Claire, but now the smiles were gone.

"Girls, don't you want to introduce Lucy and Lisa to Claire? Edith asked, smiling. "This is Lucy," said Anna in a deadpan voice void of all emotion.

"This is Lisa," said Anabel exactly the same way her sister did. *God, even their voices are identical*, Claire thought.

"Nice to meet you, Lucy and Lisa," said Claire, shakily, clearly unnerved. She then looked down at the dolls, anything to keep her from having to look into those dark black eyes. She quickly noticed that the doll Anna held must have had its arm damaged at one time, for it seemed someone had sewn it back on with what looked like a strong thread of some sort. "What happened to Lucy's arm? It looks like it was injured."

"Daddy hurt Lucy," said Anna, monotone.

"Mommy said fishing line can fix any problem," said Anabel.

"So, Mommy fixed Lucy," said Anna. Now, both girls were picking up each other's sentences faster and faster.

"So, Lucy fixed Daddy," said Anabel. "By killing Daddy," said Anna.

For a minute, no one spoke. No one made a sound. Claire couldn't speak, and Edith looked stunned beyond belief. The twins just stared expressionless at Claire.

"How dare you! How dare you say that about your father!" exclaimed Edith, who was gasping for breath. "Don't you ever say such horrible things!"

Betsy, apparently thinking all the noise was some sort of game, decided to join in by grabbing poor Lucy's head in her mouth. Anna, seeing Lucy's head suddenly disappear into Betsy's mouth, tried to save her doll by pulling as hard as she could. For a moment, it was an epic battle, girl versus pig, pig versus girl, and then all of a sudden, Anna was flying freely backward, smashing into her sister, causing both of them to land hard on the ground. Anna quickly recovered and looked down at Lucy still in her hand. Well, at least what was left of Lucy—her head was now completely gone.

"Aaahh!" screeched Anna, who then looked up at Besty, who decided at that exact moment to swallow.

"Aaahh!" screeched everyone this time. Having heard the commotion, John and Earl came running around the corner just as Betsy finished her meal.

"What happened?" asked Earl, seeing everyone in a panic. John took a quick survey of the area, looking for an enemy while dropping into a defensive posture.

"John, Besty ate Lucy's head, Do something quick!" exclaimed Claire. She was praying that John could help.

"W-what? Whose head? Who is Lucy?" asked John, completely at a loss as to what the hell was going on.

"Lucy is Anna's doll. Betsy bit off her head and swallowed it!" Claire said, frustrated at John. At least until she realized there was no way John could have known who Lucy was and the absurdity of what John could actually do to get the head back. Then to Claire's absolute horror, she started giggling uncontrollably like some kind of idiot. She tried as hard as she could to stop, but the whole situation kept playing out in her head, and she just couldn't stop laughing.

"Well, there ain't nothing to do about it now. Just got to wait it out a couple of days for a good old bowel movement, then we'll have the head back," added Earl, who also started to laugh. Anna and Anabel definitely were not finding anything funny about the situation at all.

Both girls turned their heads slowly to look Claire in the eye.

"You will get Lucy's head back now," said Anna, causing the laughter to stop abruptly.

"You will fix her," said Anabel, again, both girls immediately picking up where the other left off. Their tempo increased each time one or the other spoke.

'You will punish the beast," said Anna. "For what it has done," said Anabel.

"You will punish the beast," said Anna again.

"Just like Mommy and Daddy were punished," finished Anabel.

"Enough!" came a piercing cry. Everyone turned around and looked at Edith, who was beyond furious.

"Don't you ever say any such things about my sweet Sarah! Do you hear me?! Your mother was a Saint!" screamed Edith at the twin girls. Then with the speed and agility that shocked everyone there, Edith darted forward and snatched the first doll out of Anabel's hand and then the headless doll out of Anna's hand. "Both of you go up to your rooms right now, and I will decide if you deserve to get these back."

For what seemed like an eternity to Claire, both the

girls and Edith just looked at each other, neither giving any ground. Claire could literally feel the tension in the air even though the girl's expressions and demeanor stayed the same. Then the girls slowly walked around Edith and went into the house. Edith started crying, and Earl gently pulled her head into his chest.

"I'm s-sorry for what Betsy did and all the trouble it caused," said John honestly.

"It's alright, John, not your fault. However, if you two don't mind, I think Edith and I will retire for the evening," replied Earl.

"Yes, of course. Thank you so much for the fishing pole and the talk," Claire offered.

John handed the fishing pole to Claire and then scooped Betsy up into his arms. Together they made an awkward departure from the couple who were still holding each other. John reached the truck before Claire and put Betsy in the cab. As Claire approached the passenger side of the car and was about to reach for the door handle, she felt a weird chill run straight through her heart. She quickly gasped for breath, and then the chill just disappeared. She turned to look back at the house, and in the very upper left-hand corner of one of the windows were two sets of eyes looking right back at her.

"S-something wrong?" asked John as he opened Claire's door for her. Claire jumped a little at the sound of John's voice and turned to see him looking down at her with a concerned look on his face. She turned quickly back to the window, but the curtains were now drawn shut and the eyes were gone.

"No," replied Claire as she got into the truck, never taking her eyes off the window. "Let's just go, please."

John looked at the house to see what had caused Claire to gasp, but upon seeing nothing, he got into the truck and started the engine. They were soon driving down the gravel road and away from Claymore's house. Neither of them said a word until the house was well out of view. "John, is it alright if I can get a raincheck on the fishing trip? I think I just want to go home," asked Claire. John must have sensed how she felt, so he didn't say anything except nod his head. They briefly stopped by John's trailer to drop Besty off, and then John drove Claire home. Neither of them said a word the entire drive to Claire's house. It was well after dark when they finally pulled up into Claire's driveway.

John got out of the truck and came around to open the door for Claire. She took John's outstretched hand to step out of the truck, and then they both walked to her porch.

"I am truly sorry tonight did not go as planned. It's just... I don't know. I can't explain it," Claire said honestly. Claire knew John was being very understanding, but she felt like she owed him some kind of explanation, especially since this was supposed to be their first real date. She honestly wanted this night as bad as he did. But how could she explain to John that two little girls gave her the heebie-jeebies?

"It's alright," John assured her.

"When you saw the girls tonight, didn't you sense or feel something odd when they looked at you? I mean their eyes, it was as if they were..." Claire stopped trying to find the right words.

"As if they were staring right at your soul?" finished John. Another one of those chills ran through Claire as she heard her thoughts spoken out loud. "Both girls have lost b-both of their parents at an early age. Sometimes eyes that have seen d-death up close change. Death changes people inside, and their eyes can re-reflect that darkness."

Claire could see that as John spoke, he did so from personal experience. *How many deaths have your eyes seen, John?* Claire thought. What about her? She has seen death up close, the murder of her partner and future husband. Did Dan's death change her inside somehow? Did her eyes show it? Are they filled with a hollowed darkness like the twins? Claire suddenly grabbed onto both sides of John's head and forced him to look her right in the eyes.

"What do you see when you look into my eyes?" she asked him suddenly, needing very badly to know the answer.

"Only their beauty. D-dont worry, you are a very good person; someone who is only filled with love," John assured her. She relaxed a little bit, and John started to pull his head away. But having another thought suddenly come to her, Claire again tightened her grip on John's head and stared him straight in the eyes. She stared at those blue eyes for a very long time, but she could not see anything dark about them. Nothing like she experienced when she had looked at the twins earlier.

"I don't see any darkness in your eyes either," Claire stated, now fully releasing John from her death grip while looking a little confused. She knew John had seen many deaths, and she also knew that he had most likely killed people. How come she wasn't seeing any darkness?

"The d-darkness is still there, unfortunately. It doesn't show in my eyes because I fight to keep it at bay. It is always a constant battle that I must fight every day. But, I think the most important reason that it doesn't show in my eyes n-now is that I have found something greater than darkness to shine through them, love. Love will always overpower darkness," John explained to Claire. He then leaned down and kissed her gently on her lips. Claire, to her own surprise, grabbed John tightly and kissed him back passionately. She really did want this! No, she really needed this. John grabbed Claire by the hips and hoisted her up into his arms, kissing her all the while.

John started making his way to the porch that led to Claire's house with her wrapped tightly around him, kissing and breathing heavily. This was just like in the movies, Claire amused.

Then they both were falling, landing hard on the porch. After a few moments of curses of pain, John was by Claire's side, asking her if she was alright.

"What happened?" asked a dazed and confused Claire. "I t-tripped on the step," replied John sheepishly.

Nope! Definitely not like the movies, thought Claire. But, despite the bruise probably now forming on her butt, she was happy. Claire reached up and grabbed John by the head, then pulled him back down to finish what they had started.

Chapter 5
Betsy's Nightlight

Betsy was resting comfortably in her cozy little bed, which was right next to her master's. Her cot had its very own special night light because she didn't like the dark, and the light always made her feel safe whenever her master was away. And so, although she was home alone at the moment, Betsy was feeling very good as she started to drift off into slumber to dream about whatever pigs dream about. Suddenly, she heard the front door open and jumped out of bed, thinking her Master had come home. She went to the bedroom doorway that led to the rest of the trailer and stopped there to look down the partly-lit hallway—most of it was shrouded in darkness. As she was still staring into the dark, there was a thud in the farthest, darkest end, followed by the sound of something rolling across the trailer floor, when a barely visible object rolled out of the darkness stopping about midway where the light from the night light began to fade. Betsy tilted her head to the side, curious about the strange happening unfolding before her, and then she realized it was a juicy-looking apple. She heard her stomach give a soft growl at the sight of the delicious-looking fruit lying there. Betsy slowly approached the mouth-watering apple and was about to grab it with her mouth when the apple slowly started to move further into the darkness.

She paused for a moment, finding all this very curious. Her eyes followed the possible path the apple had taken, but her eyes were met with darkness—darkness that she was afraid of. So, deciding to wait for her master, she turned around to head back to her soft cot. However, another growl from her stomach made her stop. She was hungry, and the apple was just there. She turned back around to face the dark and proceeded after the apple anyway. Betsy was fully in the darkened hallway and sniffed around with her snout to find the apple now hidden from sight. Finally, she found the apple and happily gulped it down.

Then all of a sudden, something was around her neck. Betsy quickly started to back up, but the unseen thing around her neck quickly tightened and started digging into her skin. Betsy, in a panic, tried to shake whatever it was off, but it instead only grew tighter. It was now cutting into her flesh; a searing pain shot through her neck and head. Then Betsy realized she couldn't draw breath and decided to run back to her room. Betsy knew all she had to do was get to her room and to her bed. She knew her bed with her night light was a safe place. It had always been her safe place. Nothing could ever hurt her there. Now in a dead run to the room, Betsy could see the light. Oh, the wonderful light! Then there was only darkness.

***

It was 3 am, and John was almost to his trailer. He knew it was wrong of him to sneak out on Claire as he did, especially after the night they had shared. Yet, John needed to check on Betsy. He didn't know what eating the doll's head would do to her and wanted to make sure she was alright. *As soon as I make sure that Betsy is fine, I will then go back and apologize to Claire,* he thought. Just thinking of Claire and the night they shared all tangled up together in the throws of passion made him turn red. He couldn't remember ever being this happy in his entire life.

The way she made him feel was beyond describable. John couldn't help but think that he was still in a coma from the explosion in Iraq and was really back at the VA. He couldn't help but think this was all some wonderful dream. *Well, if this is a dream, then I don't ever want to wake up,* John thought to himself.

Smiling, he pulled up to his trailer and immediately stopped, killing the truck lights and turning off the engine. The trailer was pitch black, and the front door was wide open. John opened his glove compartment and pulled out his 1911 service pistol and a small flashlight. He quickly jumped out of his truck and started running—but not toward the trailer. Instead, he ran off into the darkness. He ran two complete circuits around his trailer to make sure there were no enemies in wait. Finally, he ran into the trailer with his gun pointed down the hallway and clicked his flashlight on. John immediately stopped in his tracks. The sound of his gun hitting the ground was deafening. He had been wrong. This wasn't some kind of wonderful dream; it was a nightmare.

***

David squatted down next to the butchered carcass lying on the ground. This was the fourth one he had found this week, and all of them had been found the same way. They all had their abdomens cut open and the organs removed. The heads had also been removed, but none of them were ever found. The heads were most likely taken as trophies to be mounted on someone's wall. David knew this was the work of poachers and the disgusted look on his face as he stood back up said exactly how he felt about poaching. David Ravenclaw was the Fish and Game Warden for this area, so he was used to seeing things like this—an unfortunate part of his job. However, he was also a full-blooded Cherokee Indian, and the ruthless destruction of any animal was a great insult to him personally. The Warden had a pretty good idea who was committing these vile acts, and looking down at the latest victim, he felt it was time he paid them a visit. David was about to get back into his truck when he heard the most God-awful scream coming from somewhere nearby. He paused for a moment to discern the direction of the scream and realized that it had come from the north; if he was right then, it most likely came from John Colt's place. He immediately got into his truck and headed in that direction. A short time later, he pulled up to John Colt's driveway and spotted John's truck parked there. He quickly got out of his truck and cautiously approached the trailer.

"Anyone home?" David called out. There was no answer, but he could make out a small light inside from one of the windows.

"John, it's me, David Ravenclaw. I heard a scream and just wanted to check if everything was alright." David called again and again with no answer. He hesitated a moment before entering the trailer, remembering the first time he had met John while on one of his patrols.

David had been tracking a wounded animal when a mountain lion had tried to attack him from behind. Just as the animal was about to jump onto his back, a knife had come sailing out of thin air and taken the lion in the neck, knocking the animal to the ground. Then, John Colt had immediately appeared out of the brush right in front of David and quickly finished the animal off so it wouldn't suffer. John had possibly saved David's life that day, for which David was eternally grateful. But it was how John had appeared seemingly out of thin air and had dispatched the mountain lion so easily that David remembered most. Seeing what John could do and then learning who John had been in the military made David a little apprehensive about going into the trailer and possibly being mistaken as an intruder. Putting his worries aside, David entered the trailer slowly and cautiously. There was John on his knees in the middle of the trailer. David immediately noticed a gun lying on the floor beside John's right hand.

David could see that John was looking at something in front of him but couldn't quite make out what it was from his position.

"John, are you alright?" David asked as he carefully approached John's right side—the side closest to the gun. John did not respond or move an inch at the sound of his voice or to his approach. He then carefully bent down and picked the gun off the ground. As David stood back up, he saw what John was looking at. On the ground in front of John lay what appeared to be a pig's body that had been crudely cut open, and its intestines spread all over the place. Blood seemed to have been smeared all over cabinets and walls. David took in the whole scene in front of him, and that's when he noticed that the pig's head was missing.

***

The lights flashed on top of the police vehicle and its sirens roared as the cruiser sped down the highway. Behind the wheel, with her hands clenched tightly on the steering wheel, was a disheveled Claire. She had received a disturbing call around 4:30 a.m. from Sallie

Mae, the dispatcher. She had told Claire that the Fish and Game Warden, David Ravenclaw, had called and said that the Sheriff was needed out at John Colt's place right away. When Claire asked Sallie Mae why the Warden needed her, she just responded that Mr. Ravenclaw didn't want to say why over the radio. Sallie Mae had also mentioned that she had already notified Deputy Jones and he was already on his way to Mr. Colt's place now. That's when Claire realized that John must have left her house soon after she had fallen asleep. She had quickly thrown on her uniform, jumped in her police cruiser, and sped off to John's place as fast as she could.

"Why couldn't Ravenclaw say what happened over the radio?" Claire asked out loud.

Her heart was racing as she pushed the gas pedal to the floor. About 20 minutes later, Claire pulled up the gravel drive to John's trailer. She could see John's truck parked near another vehicle—most likely the Warden's truck—as well as her deputy's police cruiser parked in the driveway. She quickly got out of her car and ran into John's trailer. As she entered the trailer, she immediately saw John sitting on his bed with his head down. Next to him was a broad-shouldered Native American in a Fish and Game uniform who, she assumed, had to be Ravenclaw. Finally, off to her right side was her deputy, Travis Jones, looking bored.

Travis Jones was a short, rotund man and was what one would call a true redneck. Dumb as a rock and as ignorant as one, the only reason that he was the deputy was that the previous Sheriff had been his uncle. Claire instantly didn't like the Deputy from the first day she had met him. But, she was stuck with him, for he was the only one that knew everything about everyone in town. She did plan on replacing him once she could find a good person to take his place. But, it wasn't her deputy or the Warden that held her attention it was John, sitting there. Then Claire's eyes went to the scene on the floor, to the bloodied mess that could only be what was left of poor Besty.

"My God!" Claire cried out, horrified. She then looked at John and started to go to him, but before she could reach him, the Warden quickly stepped in front of John blocking her path.

"Sheriff Davis, I presume? I am David Ravenclaw, the Fish and Game Warden. I don't think we have met,"

David said to Claire as he offered his hand. Claire, ignoring the outstretched hand, tried to get past the Warden. He, however, stopped Claire by gently grabbing her shoulder. "Sheriff, I think Mr. Colt still needs a few moments. Can we please talk privately in the kitchen?"

Looking at John, who just sat there unmoving with his eyes on what was left of Betsy, Claire jerked herself out of the Warden's hands but did allow the Warden to lead her to the kitchen area. Claire kept looking back over her shoulder toward John, but David made sure to stay between her and John as they reached the kitchen.

"Sheriff, if I may be so bold, your deputy here has informed me that you know Mr. Colt more personally," David said as delicately as he could. Claire shot Travis a scathing look, who just brushed the look off and headed for John's refrigerator.

"I know you want to be there for him, but now isn't the right time. A man like Mr. Colt handles something like this a lot differently from how other people would handle it. It's best to give him some time and space," David continued.

"What do you mean a man like him? What exactly are you trying to imply?" Claire responded, her temper starting to rise. How dare this man think he knew John better than her.

"I think you know exactly what I mean, Sheriff. Look, I am not the enemy here. I only came to help," replied David, trying to calm an agitated Claire down.

"Why exactly are you here, Warden? Was this some kind of animal attack? If it was, shouldn't you be out there finding the damn beast that did this?" Claire shouted in David's face.

"Wow! Someone's got her period early," said Travis as he sat down at the little dining table, unloading a bunch of food. This time both David and Claire shot Travis a dirty look, but again the Deputy just ignored them both.

"Sheriff, I am here because I was investigating a similar incident not too far from here when I heard a loud scream and came to investigate. When I got here, I found John on his knees, and this," he paused to pull out John's gun from his belt and proceeded to hand it to Claire, "was lying on the ground beside him. Then I saw Betsy on the ground and immediately called your office."

"But, why call me if this was an animal attack?" asked Claire, now more confused than angry. None of this made any sense.

"It wasn't an animal attack. The abdomen and intestines were cut open, not torn. The head was also cut off, not chewed. The head is also nowhere to be found," replied David.

"You mean someone deliberately came in here and did this? On purpose?" asked a stunned Claire. "Why would anyone do this? For what reason?"

"My guess would be the poachers I have been looking for. I have recently found four other animals killed in a similar fashion this week, right around this area. The poachers usually take the organs to sell them on the black market and keep the animal's heads as trophies," the Warden apprised her.

Claire sensed that David wasn't telling her the whole story, but her attention was on her stomach at that moment. It churned at the thought of the vile acts done to poor Betsy.

"Do you have any idea who these poachers are?" Claire asked, recovering quickly and her tone now very even.

"I am not sure, but I believe it may have been Toby Harnet and his lot. They have been seen around these parts a lot lately."

Claire had heard of Toby and his friends but never had met any of them yet. Toby was reputed to be the town bully who often started many of the town's bar fights. In fact, anything bad that happened in town seemed to always be linked to this Toby guy. At that moment, John stood up and slowly walked over to Betsy's body, then, kneeling down, he gently picked it up. He then slowly rose and walked out of the trailer, carrying what was left of Betsy in his arms. Claire started to go after him, but the Warden again stopped her and shook his head. Claire let John go knowing that the Warden was right.

"Ya know, I don't really see what the big deal is. Now that the retard's pig girlfriend is dead, you have him all to yourself, Sheriff," Travis let out an obscene laugh as he went back to the refrigerator to get a drink. When he came back out of the refrigerator, he felt a crushing pain starting from his nose and radiating through his entire head. Seeing bright flashes of light, Travis fell hard into the refrigerator and then to the ground. He could feel his warm blood running freely out of his nose and into his mouth. Dazed, he looked up and saw Claire standing over him, rubbing her fist.

"What the fuck you do that for?"

"If you ever talk like that to me again, it will be the last thing you ever say," Claire said in a deadly tone, then stormed out of the trailer without another word.

"Sheriff! Wait, there is something else I need to tell you," David called as he quickly followed Claire out of the trailer.

"I'm sorry, Warden, but I think I have had enough excitement for one night," replied Claire walking quickly to her car.

"This wasn't just a typical poaching incident; it was personal," called out David. This revelation made Claire halt and then turn around to face the Warden.

"The other animals had their heads cut off with a sharp knife. John's pet had its head removed by something other than a knife. It was something crude that had torn into the flesh. Then, there is the matter of the blood from the body. Usually, when an animal is killed, the blood just pools under the body. However, the blood from John's pet was purposely smeared all over the trailer. If I had to guess, I would say someone was trying to leave a message."

"Who? Toby and his friends?" asked Claire, horrified that someone did this purposely to John.

"Maybe. Like I said, they have been seen a lot in this area lately and are known to do stupid stuff like this. I have also heard rumors that every time John goes into town, Toby is usually there giving him a hard time," replied David. He paused for a moment, then made sure he had Claire's full attention before continuing. "I honestly don't know who did this to John's pig, but I would strongly recommend you find them before John does."

"Do you think John even knows that someone did this on purpose? That this was a message to him?" asked Claire, deeply concerned.

"Oh, he knows. Like I said, Sheriff, you better find them first."

THE TWINS

***

Edith awoke early in the morning to a noise coming from downstairs. She thought she had heard light footsteps and giggling. Getting out of bed and putting on her robe, she went to investigate. She slowly opened her bedroom door and looked down the hallway, but everything was dark and quiet. Then, she made her way to the landing and peered down the stairs into the darkness. Suddenly, she heard the giggling again, but it was coming from down the hall where the twin's bedroom was. Edith crept down the hall, trying not to make a noise as she went. When she finally reached the twin's bedroom door, she slowly put her ear to it.

"Lisa and Lucy want to play. Lisa and Lucy will make you pay," came from the other side of the door.

Edith reached up and gently grabbed the doorknob. She slowly turned it and gently pushed the door open. She had expected to catch the girls playing instead of sleeping. However, when she opened the door, all she saw in the night light was both of the girls asleep in their own beds. Maybe she was getting old and just hearing things, thought Edith. She watched the girls sleep for a while; they looked so content. The innocence they gave off in sleep, peaceful and serene, made Edith think about the events that had happened with Betsy. Maybe she had overreacted by yelling at them and taking away their dolls, she thought to herself. Edith remembered that she, too, had a doll as a little girl; it used to be her best friend. What if Betsy had done that to her? How would she have felt seeing Betsy eat its head? Still, the things the twins had said disturbed Edith badly, something was definitely wrong with the girls, and she decided that she would find out what it was. Gently shutting the bedroom door, she went downstairs and began making breakfast for everyone. While Edith made breakfast, she also made a picnic basket for an afternoon picnic with the girls at her 'special place.' There she would find out what was really troubling them.

About an hour later, Edith called everyone down for breakfast. Earl was the first to come down and take a seat. Edith took one look at him, noticed his bloodshot eyes, and knew that he had not slept very well.

"What's wrong? Your eyes look like a poor basset hound," she asked. Rarely did Earl ever come to breakfast looking like he hadn't slept in days.

"I didn't sleep well last night. I thought I heard a loud scream in the middle of the night. At first, I thought it may have been a coyote or some other poor animal. However, the more I thought about it, the more it sounded inhuman. Gave me some very unpleasant dreams after that. Dreams of two sets of eyes staring at me out of the darkness," Earl replied, letting out a large yawn that ended with a little shake.

Edith brought over a pot of fresh coffee and poured some into Earl's cup. Leaning down, she gave him a light kiss on the top of his head and went back to setting the table. She called up to the twins one more time as she herself finally sat down to eat. The twins came into the kitchen with their heads down, not saying a word. They both quickly took their seats but did not touch their food.

"Well, look at the two of you. Both of you look sadder than Earl does every time he goes fishing and doesn't catch anything," Edith said to the girls trying to lighten the mood. Earl stopped mid-bite into his eggs at Edith's jest of him not catching any fish.

"It's not my fault the fish ain't biting every time I go," he mumbled to himself as he finished the rest of his eggs. Edith ignored her husband's ramblings and got up from the table. She went to one of the cabinets above the stove and opened it. She pulled out the twin's dolls and brought them over to the table, then sat back down.

"I am going to let your girls have your dolls back, providing we don't have any more of the outburst the two of you had yesterday," said Edith, then she placed each doll down in front of the twins. "I am truly sorry about Lucy, Anna. The next time I go into town, I will go to the thrift store and see if I can fix her."

"Thank you, Grandma," both girls responded in a tone that was completely devoid of any emotion. They grabbed their dolls, put them on their laps, and began eating the breakfast that had been laid out before them.

Breakfast went off without any problems from the girls. In fact, Earl actually got the twins to laugh a couple of times. After breakfast, Earl went to take care of some chores, and Edith loaded up the picnic basket while the twins played in the living room. A short time later, Edith and the twins were off to Edith's 'special place' for a wonderful picnic. The trio arrived at the garden around noon, and Edith had to pause, as she always did, to take in all the beautiful flowers. There were all kinds of flowers perfectly placed all around the garden, and they were all in full bloom giving the observer a rainbow of colors. There were also stone angel statues of various sorts strategically placed throughout the garden. It had taken a couple of years to find all the statues Edith wanted for her garden and now, looking at them among the rows of flowers gave her a warm feeling all over. It was as if the stone angels were real, and they were all with her right then, watching over her.

"Well, what do you young ladies think?" Edith asked, smiling.

"It is very nice, Grandma," replied the girls unenthusiastically.

"Close your eyes and take a deep breath," said Edith, a little annoyed that the girls weren't more excited. She then closed her eyes and took a long deep breath. "Do you smell all the different flowers?"

"Yes, Grandma, they smell great," responded the twins, still unenthusiastically.

Edith opened her eyes and led the twins over to the gazebo now covered in red roses. She laid out a very large blanket and put the picnic basket down in the middle. Next, Edith opened the basket and started pulling out an assortment of snacks. There were finger sandwiches, freshly-picked blueberries, peaches, and of course, some cobbler. When Edith was done laying out all the food, she had the girls sit down, and they all began to eat. The twins ate the food mechanically, almost as if they were only eating to please their grandmother. Edith spent the time while the twins ate, educating them on the various types of flowers surrounding them. She also told the story of how Earl had surprised her with the garden for their anniversary. Finally, after she finished all her stories, she decided to talk to the girls so she could figure out what was wrong with them.

"Did you girls know I used to have a doll just like yours, and she was my very best friend," Edith began. Both girls instantly seemed very interested in this new revelation, and Edith felt she was on the right track now.

"What was her name?" asked the twins in unison.

"Her name was Mary Ann and we went everywhere together. There was never a time that Mary Ann left my side. She was someone with whom I could share all my everyday experiences, both good and bad. She was also someone with whom I could share my deepest secrets," Edith told them as she drifted down memory lane.

"What secrets?" asked Anna.

"What did you do?" asked Anabel.

"Why did you do it?" asked Anna.

"Did you get in trouble for what you did?" asked Anabel.

"What? I didn't do anything. No. Wait, what?" replied a flustered Edith, who was caught off guard by the rapidly fired accusations.

"But, you said you had secrets?" accused the twins in unison.

"The secrets are not the point of the story," responded Edith a little sourly, not liking having her flow interrupted nor being made to feel like she had committed a crime. "The point I was trying to make is that Mary Ann was everything to me and was always there for me when I needed her the most. At least that was until one day I lost her."

"Why did you lose her?" asked Anabel.

"Did she do something wrong?" asked Anna.

"Why didn't you forgive her?" asked Anabel.

"She loved you, and you lost her!" exclaimed Anna.

"Stop!" exclaimed Edith, not knowing what the hell had just happened and how in the hell she had lost control of the situation so rapidly. "Please, no more questions. Just listen to the story."

"Sorry, Grandma, please continue," responded the girls. Edith took a moment to regain her composure and began again.

"As I was saying, I had lost her and never saw Mary Ann again. I was deeply depressed for many months after that and thought many times that I couldn't continue living without her in my life. That's when I found God; He showed me that the things we love will come and go in our lives. He showed me that even though they are gone here, they are never truly lost to us. You see, when our loved ones leave us here, God takes them up to heaven, where they are happy and safe. I am telling you this because someday, you may lose Lucy and Lisa, but you must know that they will never truly be gone. Just like your Mommy and Daddy, who loved you both very much, are not truly gone. Your Mommy and Daddy are safe up in Heaven now, and they are both happy. Just like my doll Mary Ann is, and one day, we will all join them so we all can be happy and safe together. So you girls never have to feel sad or upset again, for someday we will all be together as one big happy family in God's house. Do you girls understand what I am saying to you?"

"Yes," said both girls. They both then got up and hugged Edith. "Don't worry, Grandma, we will make you happen again very soon."

Edith hugged the twins tightly, feeling that her conversation with them went very well. In fact, she felt she had really gotten the twins to understand. What she didn't see was the girl's faces as they hugged her.

***

Claire spent her day in her office going through her everyday paperwork, trying to take her mind off last night's events. Just outside her office sat Deputy Jones at his desk, applying an ice pack to his now bandaged broken nose. When Travis had come into work that afternoon with his nose bandaged and bruises under his eyes, Claire felt bad and thought of apologizing. But then she quickly remembered what the bastard had said and instead just gave him a look that told him she wasn't sorry at all. Still, she would have to find some way to get along with him since he was her only deputy, and she needed him. The people of the town didn't take too keenly to Claire when she had first arrived, partly due to her being a woman and partly due to her being city folk. That's where Travis had been somewhat of an asset, for when he went on patrol with her, the town folk were much nicer to her. But she had bigger problems to worry about for now.

After leaving John's trailer, Claire had gone to Toby's residence as soon as she had gotten back to town, but no one was home. So she had come right to her office instead of going home and getting some much-needed rest. She had tried to convince herself that she really wasn't that tired. The truth was she was completely exhausted, but John didn't have a home phone, only a hand radio in his trailer. So she came back to the office, hoping he would call in. No such luck, though, for it was already 2:30 pm, and the radio remained silent.

"Why won't you let me be there for you, John?" she whispered to herself. She knew why. It was because he was a stubborn ass that liked playing the role of a macho dumbass, that's why. *Why did you have to take me fishing? If we hadn't gone over to the Claymores to get that stupid fishing pole and fishing line, then none of this would have happened.* Claire suddenly froze and didn't breathe. She could hear David Ravenclaw's words ring out loud in her head.

"The other animals had their heads cut off with a sharp knife. John's pet had its head removed by something other than a knife. It was something crude that was torn into the flesh," the Warden had said.

"Something other than a knife," Claire repeated out loud. Then she remembered the last part David had told her.

"Then, there is the matter of the blood from the body. Usually, when an animal is killed, blood just pools under the body. However, the blood from John's pet was purposely smeared all over the trailer. If I had to guess, I would say someone was trying to leave a message."

Claire's heart jumped and started beating hard in her chest as she saw in her mind two sets of eyes staring at her from a window.

***

Edith awoke to a noise. It sounded like light footsteps and giggling again. Sitting up, she looked over at the clock on the nightstand. It was 12:00 in the morning. Groggily she wiped the sleep from her eyes and listened for the noise she thought she had heard. But, after a few moments, the only sound she could hear was Earl's snoring. A sharp poke in Earl's ribs caused him to make a few choking noises, then he rolled over, and the snoring stopped. Pleased with herself, Edith started to lay back down and continue her wonderful dream of brightly colored flowers when she heard the faint sounds of giggling again. Getting out of the bed and putting on her robe, she opened her bedroom door and peeked outside. The hallway was dark, and she didn't hear anything. Thinking the girls were playing around instead of being in bed like they were supposed to, she went to their room to check on them. As Edith approached the twin's room, she heard giggles coming from somewhere downstairs. She immediately turned back to the stairs; looking down them, all she could see was darkness. Pausing, she thought about turning the lights on but then decided to sneak up on the girls, who obviously were downstairs up to no good. Edith started slowly making her way down the stairs in the dark, making sure to hold tightly to the rail. As she slowly came down the stairs, the giggles became louder. *Well, we will see how much they giggle when I catch them in the act*, Edith thought to herself. She smiled to herself and proceeded down the stairs. Then all of a sudden, the hand she was holding the rail with came across something wet and slippery. She quickly pulled her hand away from the rail, then something tightened around her ankle, and she stumbled forward. All Edith knew was that she was falling, tumbling down the stairs. She rolled a couple of times, then came to a crashing stop at the bottom of the stairs hitting the floor hard. There was tremendous pain as she fell, but now lying on her back at the bottom of the stairs with her eyes closed, she couldn't feel anything. Then her heart suddenly pounded in her chest. She just couldn't feel anything; she couldn't move at all!

Edith opened her eyes and immediately saw two sets of eyes right in front of her face.

"Don't worry, Grandma, we are going to make you happy soon," came the whisper as Edith slipped into unconsciousness.

Chapter 6
Messages

Earl was sitting in the ER anxiously waiting to get word on how Edith was doing. It had been a couple of hours since Edith was brought in, and no one had yet come to let him know what was happening or how she was doing. The waiting was starting to get to him. Both his heart and his mind were racing. His mind kept playing out all the worst-case scenarios, and they all ended with Edith dead.

"What were you doing going downstairs at that time in the morning, and why didn't you turn on the damn lights to see what the hell you were doing?" Earl asked out loud to no one.

The twins, who were playing nearby with their dolls on the floor, gave a quick glance at Earl and went back to playing. At least they had appeared to be playing. An outside observer would have noticed how the twins would talk to their dolls and then look at Earl, nodding their heads. Earl didn't notice; his mind instead kept playing out the events that led him to find Edith at the bottom of the stairs. He had awakened to a loud crashing noise outside his room.

He looked over to see that Edith was not in bed with him. Then he jumped out of bed and ran out of the bedroom into the hallway as fast as his aging bones would allow. Clicking on the hallway light as he went, Earl quickly reached the stairs where he had thought he had heard the noise come from. Looking down the stairs, he could see Edith in her nightgown, lying flat on her back with the twins standing over her prone form.

"Quick, Grandpa! Grandma has fallen down the stairs!" exclaimed the twins in unison as they looked up at Earl.

Earl had hurriedly made his way down the stairs as fast as he could. He then dropped to his knees, causing a loud popping sound in both of them as pain shot up his legs. Earl remembered not caring about the pain, only just about Edith lying there deathly still. He had tried asking Edith if she was alright, but he got no response. Her eyes had been closed and her body very still, so much so that Earl feared that she was dead. Earl had quickly put his ear to Edith's chest, there was a heartbeat, and she was still breathing. At that moment, he had taken a deep breath and thanked God, and then he had quickly called 911. Earl remembered that the paramedics took so long to get there that he was sure Edith would be dead before they got there.

The small town where Earl and Edith lived only had a small clinic with one doctor. The clinic and the doctor, Dr. Dan Meyer, were only capable of handling small health issues. Any real serious medical issues had to be handled at St. Joseph, which was about 45 minutes away from them. This was one of the many downsides to living in such a small rural town. If you had a serious medical issue that was life-threatening and needed to be treated immediately, you were pretty much on your own.

After Edith had been loaded up into the ambulance, she was rushed to St. Joseph Hospital in St. Louis for treatment. Once Edith was taken away, Earl had quickly packed a suitcase of essential things he thought Edith would need and then rounded up the twins and rushed to the hospital where Edith had been taken. When he arrived, Edith had already been taken to the Emergency Room. An attendant brought Earl and the twins to the waiting room, then told him someone would be with him shortly.

"Earl!" came a cry that brought Earl out of his darkened thoughts. He looked up to see Claire in uniform running toward him, and then she was hugging him.

"Oh God, I'm so sorry! I heard it over the radio and got here as soon as I could. How is she? Is she alright?" asked Claire, not letting go of Earl. In fact, Claire's hold got even tighter, and Earl soon found himself fighting to get air.

"Can't breathe!" Earl gasped, and Claire immediately let him go. "I'm sorry!" Claire said apologetically.

"That's alright, dear. I know you are just worried. We all are." Earl said, comforting her, then he reached out and grabbed Claire's hands with his own.

"Have you heard anything? Is Edith alright?" Claire asked, calming down some at the comfort of Earl's grasp.

"No, it's been a couple of hours, and no one has told me what's going on. All I know is that I heard a loud crash and found Edith lying at the bottom of the stairs. Anna and Anabel were by her side, trying to help her. Poor angels must have also heard the noise and tried to help poor Edith," stated Earl.

Claire gave a wary glance at the twins playing on the floor, and her body gave a quick shake. They both looked up at her and smiled.

"Do you want me to find out what's going on for you?" began Claire, not wanting to look at the twins.

"That won't be necessary, Sheriff. Mr. Claymore, I am Doctor Hallaway, the ER doctor on duty," said a voice. Both Earl and Claire turned to see a middle-aged African American man in scrubs, with a stethoscope around his neck, approach them both. The doctor reached out to shake both Earl's and Claire's hands.

"Is she alright? Is my Edith alright?" asked Earl, not letting go of the Doctor's hand. "Can we please talk alone?" asked the Doctor, who gave Earl a look and then looked at the twins sitting on the ground playing with their dolls.

"Go ahead. I will stay with the girls," Claire offered.

Earl nodded to Claire silently, thanking her. She smiled back, letting him know it was alright. Both men then walked a little down the hallway until they believed they were far enough away from the twins that the girls wouldn't be able to hear their conversation.

"Mr. Claymore, your wife took a nasty fall down the stairs and has broken her neck. The break has severed her spinal column. I am afraid she is paralyzed from the neck down," said the Doctor gravely.

"My God!" exclaimed Earl.

His stomach churned and his knees became very weak. Earl started to fall as his knees buckled. Doctor Hallaway quickly grabbed hold of him and helped him to a nearby chair. Earl sat down heavily, trying to take it all in. The doctor gave Earl a few moments to calm down before continuing with more bad news.

"Mr. Claymore, unfortunately, that's not all. Your wife has also suffered a serious stroke which has affected her mental state negatively," finished the Doctor. Earl dropped his head into his hands and started to cry. It was all too much to take in.

THE TWINS

"Isn't there anything you can do for her, Doc?" Earl begged in between sobs.

"I'm sorry, but I'm afraid all we can do now is try to make her as comfortable as we can." replied the doctor.

"Can I see her?" asked Earl, getting up and quickly wiping the tears from his eyes. "Yes, of course! I will warn you, though, that she doesn't seem to be comprehending anything around her at the moment and she also isn't really speaking," cautioned the Doctor. Earl rose, then started to follow the doctor when all of a sudden he remembered Claire and the twins.

"Just a second, Doc, I need to let Claire know that I am going to see Edith," he said, already starting to walk back to Claire and the twins.

"If you want, you can take the twins to the waiting room around the corner so both you and the Sheriff can see Edith," offered the Doctor.

"Thank you, Doc, that sounds like a lovely idea," replied Earl.

"Great! Your wife is in room 207. I will check in with you after I do my rounds."

***

Claire sat down as Earl and the Doctor moved down the hall. They stopped just out of ear reach and started conversing. Claire leaned toward them, trying to catch their conversation. She knew that eavesdropping was wrong, but the detective in her couldn't help herself. After a few moments of being unsuccessful, she gave up. She turned to check on the girls, and there they were, standing only inches from her face. The dark pools of their eyes, staring right at her. Claire almost jumped out of her seat and had to stifle a scream. How in the hell did they sneak up on her like that! Worse, how long were they standing there that close to her? None of those thoughts did anything to calm her down.

"Don't worry, Claire, Grandma, will be alright," said Anna flatly.

"Yes, Grandma will be happy soon," said Anabel in the same tone.

"Yes, Lisa and Lucy will take care of her," said Anna.

"Forever," finished Anabel.

Then both girls held up their dolls in front of Claire's face. She didn't know what it was, the twin's eyes, their demeanor, the way their voices were emotionless when they talked, the dolls, or all of it combined, but she just wanted to get the hell away from them.

"Yes, I am sure Edith will be fine. Why don't you girls go back over there and continue playing with Lisa and Lucy? Your grandpa will be back shortly and we can all go see Edith," Claire said shakily.

The twins looked at Claire a few moments longer, and then they went back to sitting on the floor a few feet away. Claire immediately started to feel better. The girls started playing with their dolls again and Claire looked back at Earl and the Doctor. Both men said goodbye to each other, and Earl started to make his way back to Claire.

"Lisa and Lucy want to play. Lisa and Lucy will make you pay," came the singing behind Claire. The words of the song were so haunting that Claire stopped breathing. She slowly turned to look at the twins and they just sat there smiling at her.

A hand grabbed Claire's shoulder, and this time she let out a scream. Jumping out of her seat, Claire turned to see Earl with a confused panicked look on his face.

"Claire! You alright?" asked Earl, just as startled by Claire's reaction as she was to him touching her shoulder.

"Yes, I just… it's nothing." Claire stammered, the twin's behaviors still unnerving her. "Are you sure? You look like you have seen a ghost?" asked a concerned Earl.

"Yes, I am fine, I swear. How is Edith?" Claire asked, both to change the subject and out of genuine concern.

"I will tell you all about it on the way to her room. The Doc says we can go see her," Earl replied. Then he proceeded to gather his and the girls' things and started off down the hall.

They all made their way to the waiting room around the corner from Edith's room.

There Earl dropped off the twins at Claire's request. When Earl questioned her about it, she just responded that it would be best if the girls waited outside until they could see Edith's state first.

Thus, as to not shock the girls, it made sense to Earl. After he made sure the girls would be alright, he and Claire went to see Edith. On the way to Edith's room, Earl updated Claire on Edith's condition, and Claire updated Earl on what had happened to Betsy. Earl just shook his head. It was just all too much.

***

The sun had just started to crest the horizon, changing the sky from black to a soft blue. The air smelled of the burning wood from the small fire pit in the ground where the fire was starting to die out until a couple of dry logs hit the pit, and the fire roared back to life. John sat back down after tossing the firewood onto the pit. He sat there looking into the flames as he had done all through the last two nights. He had buried Betsy, or what was left of her, in the woods not too far away. The night Betsy was brutally murdered, John had carried her body in his arms for almost 2 hours before reaching what had been their favorite camping spot. He had dug a grave and made a marker out of some dead wood for Besty's final resting place. He had decided to stay there a couple of days to be with her while she made her journey to the other side. John had never really been the religious type. As a child, he hadn't put too much faith in a God that allowed his father to beat him repeatedly. As an adult in the military, where his job was to kill people on a regular basis, he didn't want to believe in God for fear of having to answer for what he had done. Then, like so many other soldiers like him, when John finally returned home from combat, he tried to believe in God just so he could be forgiven for his sins. It seemed so strange to John how one life experience can change one's view on everything. For example, John had lost so many loved ones that he had become comfortably numb to the whole experience, completely devoid of any emotion. Yet, after being with Claire for only a short time and seeing life through her wonderful eyes, his heart had finally learned to cry out, not just at the loss of Betsy but for everyone he had ever lost. Thinking of Claire brought back the image of her face as she had entered his trailer that night and seen him, then Betsy. So much emotion, so much sadness, and love were clearly displayed all over her face. It was apparent that all she had wanted to do was go to him, hold him and comfort him. But, like a complete idiot, John just couldn't let her do it, at least not then. At that moment, unknown to those around him, John had been in an intense unseen battle with the *Darkness* that resided deep within him. *Darkness* that wanted to lash out at the world and everyone around him. At that moment in the trailer, the *Darkness* wanted to find the bastards that had killed Betsy and make them suffer in such a way that would make people scream in horror after seeing what had been done to them. John felt the *Darkness* immediately rise within him again at his now darkening thoughts, and he had to strain hard to calm back down. Then a call rang out in the distance, quickly bringing John back out of his thoughts. He sprang immediately into action, putting out the fire with his water jug and disappearing into the brush. After about ten minutes, footsteps could be heard coming up the trail.

"John, are you up here?" came a man's voice. "John, it's David Ravenclaw! Are you up here?"

The Warden came around the bend and into the small camp. He looked around the landscape and then moved over to the now extinguished campfire. Bending down, he felt around the pit, noting that some of the wood was still warm and some were wet with water, which meant the owner had recently been here. Sighing, David stood back up and again looked around. "What the hell? Am I supposed to chase this guy all over the woods just to relay a message from Claire?" asked the Warden to no one in particular, then he kicked the firepit.

"What was the message?" came a whisper so close to the Warden's ear he could feel the owner's breath. In a panic, he started to run forward but ended up tripping over one of the logs from the fire pit and landed flat on his face. He tried to scramble to his feet quickly, all the while spitting dirt and leaves out of his mouth. He turned around to see John standing where he had just been standing with a small smile beginning to grow on his face.

"That's not funny! I don't care what special ops, ninja skills you have; if you ever do that to me again, I will kill you!" sputtered the Warden, still spitting dirt and wiping his mouth with his sleeve.

"My sin-cere a-apologie-es, Warden, I keep forgetting you have a bad habit of letting predators s-sneak up on you," replied John, referring to the mountain lion incident that John had saved the Warden from.

"Yeah? Well, I am going to start carrying a gun and start shooting at everything that moves. How about that?" replied the Warden, now slapping the dirt from his clothes.

"No, that won't do. You w-would most likely end up s-shooting yourself. Maybe you should take up a much less dangerous p-profession like being one of those Native American tour guides that tell of the ancient ways," replied John, giving the Warden another small smile.

"Ah, racism from a dumbass redneck, nice," replied the Warden, who was now also smiling. Both men then came together, shaking each other's hands in a proper greeting.

"W-what brings you all the way up here, David?" asked John, now that both men were done with their boyish fun. Suddenly the Warden's face immediately grew grim at the news he was about to give.

"What's wrong?" asked John, no longer smiling.

"Claire called my radio looking for you since you never went back home. She has been trying to give you your space to mourn and all, but not knowing if you were alright has really been hard on her. She is a good woman, you know," started the Warden. But John sensed that Claire being upset wasn't what made him come looking for him. He sensed that something worse had happened, and the Warden was reluctant to tell him. Thinking the worst, John tightly grabbed the Warden by the shoulders and looked him in the eyes.

"What's wrong? What really happened that m-made you come after me. What is the message?" asked John in such a tone that made the Warden try to squirm his way out of John's powerful grip. Both men were about the same height, but the Warden was of a stockier build. However, at that moment, John was proving to be the stronger of the two. When the Warden did not immediately respond, John gave him a quick shake.

"It's Mrs. Claymore. She took a bad spill down the stairs and broke her neck. The doctor said she is paralyzed from the neck down. He also said she had suffered a stroke, and her mind is gone," blurted the

Warden. John let go of him and turned away, putting his hands on his hips with his head down.

"Look, I didn't want to tell you due to recent events. I didn't want to add any more stress to you. However, Claire threatened to arrest me if I didn't track you down and tell you. I know the Claymores have been family to you. I am truly sorry to bring this to you now."

The Warden was worried that all this was too much for John to handle. He had been friends with John for a while, often going on fishing trips together. However, during those trips, John always kept any subject from getting him to open up about his past. He, respecting that, never pushed John. However, he could tell that John had demons that haunted him. Because of that and the explosion that had rocked John in Iraq, the Warden didn't really know how much stability John had.

"Thank you, I-I know you didn't have to g-get involved, and I appreciate what you have done," replied John sincerely. He then went over to his fire pit, made sure it was fully out and started off down the trail.

"Wait! Where are you going?" called the Warden.

"To buy a pie," was all that John said.

***

Claire came back into Edith's room at that hospital. She had excused herself shortly after she and Earl had arrived to see Edith for a couple of reasons. One was to give Earl a few moments alone with his wife. Claire could see he was trying really hard to keep it together in front of her, so she wanted to give him the time he needed to let his emotions out. The other reason was that she wanted to find a way to let John know what had happened to Edith. The Claymores were the closest thing to family John had, and she was certain that he would want to know about this. Claire also felt a little guilty because she was also trying to find him for her own selfish reasons. So Claire had called Sallie Mae over her radio and had asked her to reach out to the Warden, David Ravenclaw, and see if he could locate John. She was relieved when Sallie Mae had patched the Warden through to Claire and the Warden informed her that he did indeed have a way of finding John. After a short conversation with the Warden, where at one point Claire had threatened to arrest him if he didn't bring John back, Claire made her way back to room

207. When Claire entered the room, Earl looked over from his seat near Edith and gave a faint smile. Earl's eyes were bright red from the crying he must have done while she had been on the radio. Claire sat down next to him and took hold of his hand, giving it a comforting squeeze. They sat that way, both of them holding each other's hands for support for what seemed like a very long time. Then a nurse and Doctor Hallaway came into the room.

"Mr. Claymore, Sheriff," greeted the Doctor as he pulled a clipboard filled with papers off the foot of Edith's bed. "This is nurse Thompson. She will be taking care of Edith's dressing and cleaning this evening."

The doctor checked some vital stats and made some notations on the clipboard before hanging it back on the bed. Then the doctor put on his stethoscope and proceeded to listen to Edith's heart and breathing. Meanwhile, the nurse went about changing Edith's dressings and after they were changed, she then started the process of giving Edith an antibacterial dry bath. The nurse raised the blanket off Edith's legs and feet. And as she was about to apply the antibacterial soap to

Edith's feet, something caught Claire's attention that made her catch her breath.

"What is that? What is that on her legs?" asked Claire, quickly coming out of her chair and pointing at a spot on Edith's ankles. The doctor came over to look at what Claire was referring to. On Edith's legs, just above the ankles, there was some bruising and a deep thin line indent. The doctor closely examined the anomalies but only shook his head.

"I don't know. She may have tripped over something as she was going down the stairs," replied the doctor at a loss.

"I've seen this before! What could she have tripped over to cause such a fine line?" asked Claire with such determination that Dr. Hallaway was at a loss for an answer and simply just shrugged.

"Sheriff, are you there? Over," came Sallie Mae's voice over the radio.

"When Edith was brought in, did she say anything? Anything at all?" Claire asked the doctor intensely, but the doctor again only shrugged.

"Sheriff? Warden Ravenclaw gave me a message, and he said it might be very important! Over," came Sallie Mae's voice again.

"Doctor! I need you to think very hard. Did Edith say anything when she came in?" Claire asked in a tone that had Dr. Hallaway more than a little concerned.

"Sheriff? It's about John. Over," came Sallie Mae's voice yet again. This time Claire didn't ignore the call. Frustrated, she ripped the radio out of its holster and squeezed hard on the talk button.

"What is it? What's so damn important?" shouted Claire into the radio, a lot harsher than she intended. There was complete silence in the hospital room and on the radio for what seemed like an eternity, then Sallie Mae finally responded.

"Uh, the Warden said he had found John, and he had let him know about Edith," replied a now timid-sounding Sallie Mae.

"That's it? That is what was so important?" replied Claire trying to keep the frustration out of her voice.

"Uh, the Warden said that John was going into town to Aubrey's to get a pie for Edith. Over," responded a hesitant Sallie Mae.

"I am still not seeing the importance of this, Sallie Mae," replied Claire, wondering if Sallie Mae had started happy hour already.

"The Warden said that he had heard that Toby and his lot were going to be at Aubrey's today. Over," replied Sallie Mae.

"Dammit!" said Claire to no one in particular. If Toby picked a fight with John in his current state, things could really get out of hand fast. Claire really didn't want to leave Earl right now and she still had more questions for the doctor, but she knew if she didn't get to Aubreys before John, there would most likely be a murder.

"Sorry, Earl, but I have to go back into town. Will you be alright?" asked Claire.

"Of course, dear! Go on. We will be alright," replied Earl. Claire was almost out of the door when the doctor's words stopped her cold.

"Sheriff! Now that I think about it, Edith did say something when she came in, but it didn't make any sense," started the doctor with confusion evident in his voice. She had said 'their eyes.'"

Chapter 7
Aubrey's

Aubrey's was a diner named after the owner, Joyce Aubrey. It was located just on the edge of town, where anyone traveling through the town had to pass by it. Aubrey's was a relatively large place where all the "real" locals went to get fresh chow. There were a few other eateries in town, but none as good or as famous as Aubrey's. From the outside, painted in alternating white and red horizontal stripes, it looked like any other diner, complete with glass windows that ran the full length of the building for the customers to see out. On top of the building, a huge sign that said, "Aubrey's, come get some!" was hoisted, which lit up at night with red lights. The inside, however, did not look anything like the typical diner, even though it did have the typical breakfast bar. The bar was solid wood stained with a clear coat that brought out the wood's natural colors. There were no sitting booths. Instead, round oak wooden tables with chairs that matched the bar were spread throughout the diner. The walls were loaded with pictures of all the town folks and their greatest moments. The diner was well known for having the best breakfast, lunch, and dinner than any other place for miles around. In fact, many people from nearby towns would make the drive just to get a taste of Aubrey's homemade cream pies. Aubrey's was, of course, well known for other things, and it wasn't food.

Nope, the other thing that people came to Aubrey's for was gossip. If anyone wanted the latest and greatest on what was going on in town or even outside of town, all they had to do was to come to Aubreys. When you live in a small town without any real excitement, one has to rely on the little things for entertainment. Today was no different, except the gossip wasn't about who was sleeping with whom. No, this time, the gossip centered around Edith's falling down the stairs and John's pig being butchered.

"That poor thing, first her daughter is murdered by that psychopath of a boyfriend, then she ends up having to raise her granddaughters, and now she is paralyzed from falling down the stairs," Mary Beth said to Dr. Dan Meyer as she poured him another cup of coffee at the breakfast bar.

Mary Beth was the diner's main waitress and hostess. She was also the main reason most of the diner's patrons were male. She was only twenty-five years old and absolutely stunning. With long strawberry blonde hair, large almond-shaped eyes, full pouty lips, a large bosom, and legs that went on forever, she was a sight to behold. Of course, Mary Beth wasn't just beautiful; she was one of the nicest people anyone could meet. All the townsfolk loved her and her beautiful spirit. A Lot of people had compared her sweetness to that of Sarah Claymore's. A comparison that Mary Beth didn't mind. In fact, she was proud of it for she remembered Sarah and had thought she was a wonderful person.

"Yep, bad luck that. Now poor Earl has to take care of Edith and the twins all by himself," Dr. Meyer said as he sprinkled salt and pepper onto his eggs. Dr. Meyer was the town's only doctor, even though he looked more like a patient. He was a short and very wide bald man that looked like he was always about to have a heart attack.

"Well, at least John Colt will help out around the farm," replied Mary Beth as she picked up another order the cook had just set up on the counter.

"Bah, if you call having a retard's help actual help," came a call followed by laughter from one of the tables. Seated on one end of the room was the town's bully, Tobi Harnet, with his two minions, Jake Nickels and Dale Brown. Tobi was a big man, both in height and in size. He was about 6'4 and weighed close to 280 lbs. He looked like a bull that had turned human. In fact, many of the townsfolk would often say that Tobi's mother had sex with a bull, and Tobi was the result of such a union. Naturally, being a big ogre with a sloping forehead, Tobi felt it was his birthright to bully everyone in town and make their life miserable.

"You be quiet, Tobi Harnet, before someone comes over there and teaches you proper respect for people!" snapped Mary Beth as she brought the tray full of food over to Tobi's table. "John Colt is a good man and has fought for his country, more than you have ever done."

When Mary Beth reached his table, she slammed his food down in front of him, causing one of the sausage links to roll off the plate. The sausage fell on

Tobi's crotch, drawing laughter from both Jake and Dale.

However, Tobi didn't find it as funny as his two minions did, especially since they were laughing at him.

"Goddammit, Mary Beth, what the hell is your problem today!" cried Tobi picking up the sausage link off his crotch and tossing it back onto his plate. "You got a thing for retards or something?"

"I must. I put up with you every day," answered Mary Beth drawing more chuckles from Jake and Dale.

"Or maybe Mary Beth just wanted you to know what it felt like to have a sausage of real size between your legs for once," offered Jake as he flashed a dazzling smile at Mary Beth.

Unlike Tobi, Jake looked like he had just walked out of one of those celebrity magazines. He had short black hair that was parted nicely on one side, bright clear blue eyes, a jawline that looked like it was chiseled out of stone, and a smile that could charm the skirt off any woman.

Well, almost any woman. Although Jake had the money and the looks, Mary Beth knew better than to fall for his antics. She knew that Jake was just as bad as Tobi, if not worse. When Mary Beth was a teenager in high school, one of the cheerleaders was badly beaten and raped. The rumor was that Jake had lured the girl to his house, where Tobi and Dale were waiting. It was believed that all three took turns beating her and raping her. When the girl had been questioned about her attackers, she had refused to say. Some say that she remained silent because Sheriff Bowman and his nephew, Travis Jones, were good friends with Dale's family and that she had been threatened into not confessing by Travis. The girl had committed suicide a couple of days later. Whether the rumors were true or not, Mary Beth didn't trust any of them, especially Jake.

"Fuck you!" exclaimed Tobi punching Jake hard in the arm and taking Jake's mirth away. "Give it up, Jake. Mary Beth isn't going to spread those purdy little legs for you no matter how much you smile at her."

"Yeah, Mary Beth is just a tease," chimed in Dale. He was the smallest of the group and looked like one of those hippie surfer types with long shaggy blonde hair.

"Ugh!" replied Mary Beth as she slammed the last two plates down in front of Jake and Dale before walking away in disgust. She returned to the breakfast bar and topped off Dr. Meyer's coffee before returning to her original conversation with the doctor. "I just find it hard to believe that Edith could have fallen down the stairs like that. I mean, she always seemed so graceful."

"They called me from St. Joseph as soon as she was admitted since I am Edith's primary physician. All they told me was they believed she fell down the stairs causing her to break her neck, paralyzing her. Apparently, the twins had found her at the bottom of the stairs, but no one knows why she was up and about at that time. Since Edith has also suffered a stroke and isn't saying anything at the moment, we may never know what actually happened," stated Dr. Meyer as he took another bite of his eggs.

"Maybe the retard did it!" shouted Tobi while laughing. "I mean, first his girlfriend 'Betsy the Pig' gets gutted and chopped up, then Mrs. Claymore apparently took a header down the stairs. Maybe your war hero has finally fully flipped his switch and is seeing everything around him as an enemy."

"Yeah, or maybe he killed the pig in the throes of passion and then decided to have a go at a real woman like Mrs. Claymore. Except she decided she didn't want anything to do with the psycho and fell down the stairs trying to get away from him!" exclaimed Dale, who got hearty laughs out of both Tobi and Jake.

"God damn it, Dale!" Mary Beth shouted. She quickly looked up to the roof and gave a quick prayer for forgiveness for taking the Lord's name in vain.

"Ding Ding," sounded the bell above the entrance door. Everyone in the restaurant turned their eyes to the front door and then there was complete silence because in the doorway stood John. He stood there for a moment with all eyes on him, and he immediately felt his anxiety levels rise sharply. Then John's eyes found the eyes of Tobi, and he could feel the anxiety being replaced by the *Darkness*. He could feel the *Darkness* growing inside him, which almost made him leave, but he had come here to get a pie for Edith and wasn't going to leave without one. Fighting back the *Darkness,* John ignored Tobi and walked over to the breakfast bar and took a seat. After a few more moments of deafening silence, Mary Beth grabbed her pen and pad and went over to take John's order.

"Hello, John! What can I get fer ya today, sweetie?" Mary Beth asked, breaking the silence which seemed to put everything back into motion as if a spell had been lifted.

"Just a p-p-peach cobbler and a c-cup of c-coffee. To go p-please," stammered John, his stuttering coming back as he tried to control his emotions.

"Oink oink," came a call from Tobi's table.

"Sure, sweetie, coming right up," said Mary Beth while throwing an angry glare at Tobi. "There is a fresh pie coming out of the oven in just a few minutes. Let me get you that coffee while you wait."

As Mary Beth went to get John's coffee, Tobi nudged Dale in his arm with an elbow giving him a knowing nod. Dale got up, then moved over by the front door and pretended to be looking at the many pictures on the wall.

"Hey, Mary Beth, can we get a big plate of bacon over here?" called Tobi with a big grin on his face.

"Yeah, can you make sure it was just freshly butchered?" added Jake. Mary Beth immediately looked over at John and she could see his knuckles turning white. She quickly made the coffee and brought it over to John.

"I am assuming you are going to visit Edith in the hospital, and that's why you are getting the pie. I know she will be very happy that you brought her a little something. Let me go check on it and get you on your way," said Mary Beth, trying to take John's mind off Tobi and also letting him know it would be best if he didn't stay too long. It was too late, though, because, at that moment, Tobi pushed away from the table and got up. He then walked slowly over to the breakfast bar next to John and leaned against it in such a way that he would be facing both John and his audience.

"Look here, y'all. Our presence is graced with a real-life war hero!" Tobi said loudly, drawing hoots and hollers from his two disciples. "Tell me, war hero, have you killed any Viet Chong lately?"

"Tobi, that's enough! Sit down and shut your mouth, or I will call the Sheriff!" yelled Mary Beth.

"Go ahead, have you seen the Sheriff? I would love to have that tight little ass come in here and give me a good old spanking," Tobi replied, drawing more hoots and hollers from his minions. Then Tobi put his hand on John's shoulder and leaned in real close to John's face.

"How about it, war hero, I heard you and the Sheriff have been playing hide the baton. How is that ass? Is it as tight as it looks?"

"Stop it!" screamed Mary Beth. Surprising herself, she ran at Tobi to smack him in the mouth, but Dale was on her in an instant. He grabbed Mary Beth from behind, pinning both her arms to her sides. Struggling as she was, Mary Beth couldn't break Dale's hold.

Jake got up from the table and slowly walked over to Mary Beth. Stopping in front of her, he reached up and moved some of Mary Beth's hair out of her eyes and stared at her intently for a few moments, and then his eyes slowly moved down her face to settle on her large breasts. Seeing where Jake's eyes were going, Mary Beth started to scream, but Dale clamped one hand over her mouth. Mary Beth again tried to struggle to escape, but Dale was a lot stronger than he looked.

"You know, Mary Beth, you have played this little cat and mouse game with me for years. I have to say that it has been fun, but we both know that you really like me and you really want to be with me in every way," said Jake, still staring at Mary Beth's bosom. He then reached up with both hands and ripped her shirt open, exposing her breasts.

Everyone was so intent on what was happening to Mary Beth that no one was paying any mind to John, who was still just sitting there. If they had noticed him, they would have seen that his hands were clenched into fists and his knuckles were completely white. They also would have noticed that John's knuckles were not the only things that had turned colors; his face was now completely red. While all the events were taking place, the *Darkness* was taking over John completely. John tried as hard as he could to win the battle with the *Darkness*, but in the end, the *Darkness* simply would not lose! John's left hand grabbed the hand Tobi had put on his shoulder and pulled it down at such an angle that forced Tobi's head to come down where it met John's right fist. Tobi felt an explosion of pain in his jaw and felt two of his teeth break free. He could also feel himself falling backward, then onto the floor. As Tobi fell to the ground, John came off the barstool just as Jake had turned around toward him. Jake's face was also met with one of John's fists, and he also went flying backward. Dale quickly let go of Mary Beth, who immediately ran and hid behind the counter, where she discovered the cook and the doctor hiding. Apparently, when the doc and the cook saw Tobi approaching the bar earlier, they had suspected something bad was going to happen, so they both hid behind the counter while no one was paying them any attention.

Dale swung a right hook at John's head, but John paired the blow bringing his elbow crashing into his opponent's nose. Blood exploded everywhere as Dale's nose broke from the blow. As Dale started falling backward, John launched a front kick into Dale's chest, sending him flying into the wall and knocking pictures to the floor. Just as he collapsed to the floor, Jake got back to his feet and charged John hoping to take him to the ground. John turned to meet the charge, and as Jake approached, John shuffled off to one side and then gave the charging Jake a shove that sent him crashing into the bar. John was on Jake in an instant, grabbing him by the hair and yanking him back up to his feet. He then grabbed Jake by the groin and began to squeeze hard. Jake screamed as unbearable pain shot through his groin and then all throughout his body. John didn't stop. He next yanked Jake's head downward to meet his incoming knee. Jake was fully out of this fight. A loud noise came from behind John as chairs were thrown out of the way.

John turned to see Tobi back on his feet, standing there smiling with blood running freely out of his mouth.

"Is that all you got, Soldier Boy? If it is, you ain't got shit!" declared Tobi, then he spat a glob of blood on the ground and waded in.

John ducked the first punch and tried to get behind Tobi, but the big man was surprisingly agile. Tobi sidestepped, spun, and delivered a left cross that landed squarely on the side of John's head. The blow sent John flying into some tables and chairs. Most men would have been out for the count after a blow like that; however, the *Darkness* wouldn't allow it. John kicked the tables out of his way and quickly got back to his feet. Tobi picked up one of the nearby chairs as John rose. Tobi threw the chair at John forcing him to duck, which is what Tobi was hoping for. The chair was never meant to hit John. It was only to make him duck down so that Tobi, who quickly followed behind, could ram his knee into John's descending face. John didn't realize Tobi's true intent until it was too late. However, as Tobi's knee came up to meet his face, John was able to get his arms up as some form of defense and turn his head so as not to have his face take the full force of the blow. Tobi was a giant man and the sheer power behind the knee was enough to break through John's defenses. The force of the blow was enough to send him flying backward into the air and landing hard against the wall. The wall shook from John's body crashing into it and several more pictures fell to the ground causing the broken glass to go everywhere.

"That's right, Soldier Boy, your ass is mine, and I'm going to butcher you just like your fucking pig!" Tobi yelled at John, who was now a crumpled heap on the floor. Just as Tobi was about to go over and finish him off, John slowly rose off the ground and climbed back to his feet. Tobi paused as John's gaze met his. He could sense something different about John; he could see it in those eyes. What Tobi had sensed was the *Darkness* that now fully controlled John.

"You are dead," The *Darkness* stated as one would state a simple fact. Then in a blink of an eye, the *Darkness* closed the distance between him and Tobi.

Before Tobi could even fathom what was happening, the *Darkness* was raining blows on him. Every punch found its mark, and the next thing Tobi knew was that he was on the ground with the *Darkness* on top of him, continuing its brutal assault. Tobi could feel his nose and then his jaw break; the pain was excruciating.

While the *Darkness* pounded on Tobi, Dale got back up on his feet. He ran and grabbed a steak knife off one of the plates the doctor had been eating off of and reversed the blade so its handle was in his hand, but the blade lay against his arm. He then slowly crept around behind John, trying to stay out of his line of sight. Which really wasn't necessary, for John was gone, only the *Darkness* was there, and it was in full attack mode. The only thing the *Darkness* attention was on was Tobi. So Dale was able to get up right behind John unchallenged. Seeing his opportunity, Dale slowly raised the knife above John's back. Just as Dale was about to bring the knife down onto John, he heard the sound of a gun being cocked. Dale froze as he felt the barrel being pressed into the back of his head.

"Drop the knife, or I swear I will send you to meet whatever God you choose," said Claire in a tone that left no doubt in Dale's mind that she would do it. Dale slowly lowered his knife, and Deputy Jones, who had come in with Claire, grabbed Dale and cuffed his hands. As Deputy Jones took care of Dale, Claire turned her attention to John, who was still beating on Tobi—Tobi was no longer defending himself, having already passed out from the pain.

However, that didn't stop the *Darkness* from continuing his assault. John's fist, now fully covered in blood, kept raining down onto Tobi's unconscious form.

"John! Stop!" cried Claire, horrified by the sight unfolding in front of her. She reached out and tried to grab John by the shoulders to get him to stop. The *Darkness,* however, spun on her, and Claire jumped back out of his reach, bringing her gun up in defense. Deputy Jones saw John going after Claire, threw a hand-cuffed Dale to the ground, and drew his own firearm, taking aim at John's head. For a moment, everyone froze, and the silence was deafening.

"John! It's me, Claire! Please stop!" Claire exclaimed, breaking the silence. Deputy Jones started to slowly move into a different position to take John down, but Claire gave him a look that told him not to move. Claire knew that John was at this moment fighting with his darker self and wasn't fully comprehending what was going on, but she had to find a way to get through to him. She slowly put her gun away and carefully approached John. He started to lunge but stopped as quickly as he started. His facial expression kept changing, only proving to Claire that she was right about him being in battle with himself. Claire reached up and gently grabbed John on both sides of his head. She tilted his head down so that their eyes were looking straight at each other, at each other's soul. The darkness quickly faded, and John came fully back. He looked at Claire with love in his eyes, then collapsed unconscious at her feet.

Chapter 8
Frightening Clues and More!

Claire watched the ambulance driver shut the ambulance doors through the large window from inside the now trashed restaurant. The other two ambulances that carried Tobi and Jake had already left. This last ambulance carried a still shaken and battered Dale. After John had passed out on the floor, Claire had handcuffed him while he was unconscious.

She knew she had gotten through to John before he passed out but thought it was safer to have him restrained just in case he woke up as something else. After John was secured, Claire had Deputy Jones call ambulances for Tobi and his crew. All of them were still alive, even Tobi, although barely. They all needed immediate medical treatment, at least according to Doctor Meyer, who finally had come out of his hiding place to look the trio over. He told Claire that Tobi needed to go into the first ambulance because he had several broken bones in his face and was bleeding internally. He also told Claire that Tobi could still yet succumb to his injuries. So Toby was the first to have been whisked away, followed by Jake and then finally Dale. Just as the final ambulance was leaving, Warden David Ravenclaw's truck pulled into Aubrey's parking lot. The Warden jumped out of his truck and watched as the ambulance drove away. Warden Ravenclaw then went into Aubrey's and was immediately assailed with the damage the brawl had left behind. The Warden saw all the broken tables, chairs, dishes, and broken glass from all pictures strewn all over the floor. Most importantly, he saw all the blood, which there was a lot of.

"Jesus, that's a lot of blood!" exclaimed the Warden. He looked over at Claire, who was standing at the window still looking out. "I take it you didn't make it here before, John?"

"Nope," was all that Claire said.

"Tobi?" Warden asked, already knowing the answer.

"Still alive, on the way to the hospital along with Jake and Dale," responded Claire, still not moving from the window.

"And John?" pushed the Warden.

"Restrained in the back of the cruiser," that was all Claire would say.

"Are you going to lock him up?" asked Joyce Aubrey.

Joyce Aubrey, the sole owner of Aubrey's, lived right behind the restaurant and came as fast as she could after being called by her cook. When she had arrived and seen her restaurant trashed she wanted to scream. Then she saw poor Mary Beth and the state she was in. Mary Beth had been sitting in a corner still crying, with a large police coat wrapped around her, provided by Deputy Jones. When Aubrey had been told about what had happened to Mary Beth, Aubrey lost it. She grabbed a broken chair leg and vowed to go after those boys and teach them what their mothers should have. Lucky for Jake, Deputy Jones intercepted Aubrey and took away her weapon. After finally calming down, Aubrey had gone to comfort the shaken Mary Beth. Shortly after that, Aubrey had the cook take Mary Beth home. Since then, Aubrey had been trying to clean up the mess as the ambulance drivers hauled off Tobi and his lot one by one.

"He tore up your restaurant and hospitalized three of your customers, one who might still die. Animals like that need to be behind bars," stated Doctor Meyer with open disgust.

"You can't arrest poor John for saving Mary Beth from being raped by those assholes. He should be given a medal, not locked up," Aubrey shot back at the Doctor.

Warden Ravenclaw knew that Doctor Meyer was most likely upset with his free breakfast being interrupted more than any feelings for Tobi and his gang getting a beat down. Still, the harsh words caused the Warden to glance at Claire. He had seen what had happened to Deputy Jones when he had said bad things about John in front of her. To his surprise, Claire just remained silent, standing there looking out the window. Then the Warden followed Claire's line of sight and saw that she had been watching John in the back of the squad car all along.

"Well, are you going to lock that monster up, or are you going to give him a medal as Aubrey suggests for beating up our citizens?" asked the flustered Doctor.

The Warden noticed how the doctor's words suggested that John was considered a dangerous outsider and not one of them. He knew that the townsfolk secretly never really considered John one of them, but hearing the words out loud just now made The Warden wince. He was about to suggest that the Doctor leave before saying something that would definitely set Claire off, but Claire finally spoke up.

"Doctor Meyer, I appreciate everything you did here with attending to Tobi and his friends' medical needs. However, I consider any man who hides behind a counter while an innocent young girl is being raped to be the biggest monster there is. As for John, he is in my custody, not yours. Therefore your thoughts on the matter are irrelevant. Your services are no longer needed. You may leave." She just kept staring out the window, looking at John as she said this.

The Doctor started to mutter an angry retort, but the Warden motioned him to leave. Finally, the Doctor threw his arms up in the air and stormed out of the restaurant.

Many moments passed when no one said anything. The only sounds were of Aubrey sweeping up broken glass. Finally, the Warden cautiously approached Claire.

"Claire? Are you alright?"

Another moment passed before Claire finally spoke, "You should have seen him, David, the way he kept beating Tobi. You should have seen him when he faced me when I had tried to stop him. It wasn't the blood sprayed all over his face and dripping from his hands that scared me; it was what I saw in him at that moment. Do you think he will always be like this?" Claire asked the Warden.

"I think his mind was broken in two pieces by his trials. Now that the trials are over, the two pieces of his mind are fighting for dominance instead of working together. Can one side win over the other? Maybe," answered the Warden.

"If one side does conquer the other, which side will win in the end?" Claire mused, still staring out the window with a vacant look.

"I think that depends a lot on you. I've seen him change since meeting you, and I honestly believe you are helping the good side win," the Warden responded.

"I just don't know if it will be enough," Claire stated distantly.

"Do you love him?" asked the Warden. Claire took a long moment to answer, surprised and shocked by the Warden's blunt question.

"Yes. I love him with every part of my being," her voice broke, and a tear ran down her cheek as she said this.

"Then you have to have faith that love does conquer all. In my lifetime, I have seen a myriad of emotions, hate, greed, envy, and so on. But, I have never seen any of them come close to the power of love. I have seen the power of love save so many people, and if you truly do love him, then I honestly believe the good side will win in the end."

"I truly hope so, it's just his eyes...." started Claire, then she stopped and sucked in her breath sharply. At that moment, she remembered the Doctor's words at the hospital. The last words that Edith had said were, 'Their eyes.' Then she remembered two sets of eyes staring at her from the bedroom window at the Claymore's farmhouse. Two sets of eyes that looked exactly as John's eyes did when Claire had tried to stop him from beating Tobi to death. The eyes of a killer.

"Claire, are you alright?" asked the Warden, who immediately grew concerned after Claire had stopped mid-sentence and gave a look as if she had just seen a ghost. Claire then turned toward the Warden to say something, but as she did, she stepped on a broken picture on the ground. She looked down, and it was a picture of Sarah, her husband, and the twins. Claire bent down and picked up the picture. In the picture, Claire could see that Sarah and her husband were smiling at the camera while holding hands. To the side of them were the twins with their dolls in their hands. Instead of looking at the camera smiling like their parents, both girls were staring at their father. Their eyes were not the eyes of a child who loved their parents; their eyes were the same as how John's had just been.

"When was this taken?" Claire asked Aubrey suddenly, ignoring the Warden's question. Claire held the picture up before Aubrey, who took a closer look at it.

"I believe that was taken about a week before the poor things' father committed suicide," replied Aubrey, saddened by the tragic event. Like so many of the townsfolk, they had all loved Sarah and had to come to love her husband, Neil. When they had learned of his apparent suicide, they had all been taken aback.

"Claire, what's going on?" asked the Warden again, even more concerned than before.

"I have to go," was all Claire said as she turned and left, leaving both Aubrey and the Warden even more confused.

***

"Yes, please have him call me as soon as he can. Yes, thank you," Claire said to the person on the other end of the phone as she ended her call. When she had gotten back to the station, she immediately reached out to the Detective that had handled the case of the twin's mother, Sarah. However, Detective Marshall was out of the office on another case at the moment. She picked up the photo of the twins and their parents, the one she had taken from Aubrey's diner. She remembered seeing a couple of photos of the twins before on the end table at Earl and Edith's house the day Edith had passed out on the front lawn. Even though she had only briefly seen the pictures, she could have sworn the twins in the photo were having fun and smiling. This photo, however, was very dark and disturbing. *What had happened to the twins that made them change?* Claire wondered.

"Sheriff, have you decided what you want to do with him?" asked deputy Jones, interrupting Claire's train of thought. Claire looked up at her deputy, who in turn nodded his head toward John, who was in the holding cell across the room. Claire looked over at John lying down on the cot staring at the ceiling. The drive from Aubrey's to the station had been a quiet one.

"You know, as long as Aubrey and Mary Beth claim John acted in self-defense, we can't hold him," said Deputy Jones. Then he gave Claire a wink. "Unless, of course, you want to make up a charge."

"Shouldn't you be out patrolling?" responded Claire, which was her way of telling the Deputy that his presence was not needed or wanted. With a shrug, the Deputy grabbed his gear and left. After Deputy Jones was gone, Claire got up and went over to the jail cell holding John. He sat up at hearing her approach, and they both just stared at each other for a while.

"I tried to give you your space. You know that, right?" said Claire, being the first to break the silence.

"I know."

"I wanted to be there for you after what happened to Betsy."

"I know," John responded again.

"Then why didn't you let me?" asked Claire, her tone bordering on accusatory.

"There is a d-darkness inside me that tries to t-take over at certain times. It is a constant b-battle that I am afraid someday I am going to lose. I am afraid if I lose, I will hurt you just like T-toby," responded John.

"I am not going to pretend I understand what battle you face, but did you ever think for once that it is a battle that you don't have to fight alone?" asked a frustrated Claire.

"No," John admitted shamefully. He had always felt this was his burden to bear and his alone.

"I love you, John. I know that now. I love you no matter what, and I have been recently informed by the highest authority, Mr. David Ravingclaw, that love will always defeat darkness," said Claire, forming a small smile. John couldn't help but smile back at the reference to the Warden. Ravenclaw was right, though; they all were. Earl, Edith, and David had been telling him all along that they all were there to help him fight his internal battle with unconditional love. For the first time, John felt he had a chance at winning just as long as he let all of them, especially Claire, in.

"Who am I to dismiss the great wisdom of D-david Ravenclaw." Stated John with mock praise getting up from the cot and walking over to Claire.

"Well, he is Native American, and they are supposed to be one with the natural order of things," responded Claire, playing along.

"Well, for one, way to s-stereotype a whole race of people. Two, even though David does f-follow the ways of his p-people he is actually from Detroit. So the only s-sage advice he has is how not to get m-mugged on public transportation," John said, laughing. Then he became serious again. He reached through the bars and took hold of Claire's hands while looking into her eyes. "I love you with every p-part of me, and I promise I will never s-shut you out again."

"No, you won't because I won't let you."

She unlocked the cell, and when John came out, the two immediately embraced each other. Then all of a sudden, Claire pushed John back and looked at him in a peculiar way.

"What's wrong?" asked John, thinking he had done something wrong already.

"Was the darkness in you always there, or is it something that came on later?" asked Claire.

"It happened when I was in the military. You are thrown into situations where fear and anxiety will get you and others k-killed. So some like me created the d-darkness because when fear and anxiety become nonexistent, we can d-do things in that state of mind that a moral conscience normally wouldn't allow.

"In the beginning, it was like t-turning a light switch on and off, but somewhere along the line, some like me l-lose control of the switch. Certain things will trigger it and then the fight for c-control of the switch begins," said John, trying to paint a picture for Claire but knowing that unless she had been through the same thing, she would never fully understand.

"So, fear and anxiety trigger it in you?"

"Yes," responded John, not understanding where Claire was trying to go with this.

"Does it have to be an emotion, or could it be an object?" asked Claire anxiously, pieces of a puzzle coming together in her mind.

"I guess it could be an object. I have s-seen soldiers use p-photos of loved ones or charms to turn on the darkness," John answered, now really confused.

"Like a DOLL? Or should I say DOLLS?" asked Claire

"I guess so," replied John, still not putting two and two together.

"We have to go, now!" exclaimed Claire. Not having time to explain just then. Without saying another word, Claire went to her desk and grabbed the photo of the twins; then, she motioned for John to follow her.

***

Earl sat in the waiting room while more tests were being performed on Edith. The nurses had informed him that it would be some time before he would be allowed to visit his wife again, so he took that time to give the twins a break from the hospital. He had taken the twins home to bathe, eat and rest before rushing back to the hospital. The twins now sat on the ground playing with their dolls being good little girls. Earl marveled at how well the girls were taking the news about Edith and how well they had been behaving for him. When he first told the girls about Edith and her condition, they had assured him that everything would be alright and that they would take care of him. Earl had smiled at the sweet jester. In reality, Earl was scared; how in the hell was he going to take care of

Edith at home since he couldn't afford to put her in a facility? How was he supposed to care for her, raise twin girls and run an entire farm by himself? Maybe he could get John and some of the townsfolk to help him out. The thought of John brought back the image of Claire rushing off to Aubrey's to prevent John from doing something stupid. Earl hoped Claire was successful because he didn't want anything bad to happen to John. He was such a good lad. Just then, there was excitement in the halls. The hospital lit up with an announcement for a "code red," and nurses started running around.

"Wonder what the hoopla is all about?" Earl said, thinking out loud. The twins just shrugged their shoulders and went back to playing.

"Mr. Claymore?" called out a voice, coming from the opposite direction of the commotion. Earl turned around to see Dr. Halloway approaching. He got up and shook the doctor's hand.

"Any news, Doc?" He did not have too much hope for a good answer. Although they had been running tests all day, he didn't think there was going to be anything positive to come from it all.

"Actually, there is some good news. Even though the tests did not show us anything we could use to improve Edith's condition, the visual exercises we gave her did get some cognitive results. In other words, she does seem to understand what is happening around her and who everyone is. She just is still having trouble putting thoughts into actual words. This means that it doesn't look like the stroke had caused any permanent memory loss and that she could be communicating with all of us again soon," The doctor assured Earl.

He was so elated by the news that he might get Edith back mentally, if not physically, that he didn't notice that the twins had stopped playing with their dolls and were paying very close attention to the conversation.

"I can't thank you enough, Doc, for bringing me such great news. Is it alright if the twins go with me this time to see Edith? I just know seeing them will bring a smile to her face," pleaded Earl.

"Of course, just know that Edith had to go through a lot today, and she is very exhausted. She is sleeping right now, so please do not wake her. Try to let her rest and wake on her own."

"Yes, sir, not a problem," responded Earl happily.

"Now, if you will excuse me, I am being paged to the ER," said the Doctor as he excused himself.

"Come on, girls, gather your things. We are going to see Grandma!" exclaimed Earl excitedly. Again so excited was he that he didn't see the looks the twin girls exchanged with each other.

***

"Wait, you are t-telling me that you think the twins had something to do with Edith's f-fall down the stairs?" asked John. Claire had filled John in on all that had happened with Claymores, from Edith's fall to her last words, "their eyes," as the two of them drove to the hospital.

"Yes," responded Claire, knowing how crazy she must have sounded when she told John her thoughts.

"That's crazy. Edith p-probably heard an animal downstairs, and when she went to investigate, she probably saw the animal's eyes r-right before she fell down the stairs," John tried to rationalize. "Besides, if they did do it, why?

"I believe it has to do with the dolls," Claire winced as she said the words out loud.

"You're telling me your theory is a c-couple of dolls had made the twins push Edith down the s-stairs?" John asked incredulously.

"No, I don't think the dolls are making them do it. I think that when something happens to the dolls that it triggers their darkness, and they act out at the individual that they felt somehow wronged them or the dolls," Claire tried to explain, but she could see by the look on John's face that he wasn't buying it.

"Think about it for a moment. Have you ever met the twins before they had the dolls?"

"A few times," John replied.

"And how were they? How did they act?" asked Claire.

"I don't know, like k-kids," John answered.

"But, they were definitely different then than they are now, correct?" Claire continued, trying to draw the picture.

"Yeah, but they are going through adolescence. All k-kids change and d-do that goth thing," reasoned John. Claire, however, wasn't done just yet.

"The day we went to the Claymore's to get the fishing pole, you didn't see how they acted when Edith scolded them the first time. I did. However, you did see them when she took away their dolls. Do you remember? More importantly, did you see their eyes and the way they looked at her?" asked Claire. When she didn't get a response from John, she glanced over at him and could see he was remembering.

"Yes," was John's only response. Claire knew she had hit on something, and John was starting to see it. Claire hesitated for a moment, knowing that what she was about to say now was going to drive the point home, but at what cost?

"I also think they had something to do with Betsy's death," blurted Claire. John went very quiet and Claire got worried she may have triggered the *Darkness*, but when she glanced over at him again, she could see that her words had caused a light to go on.

"Can't be," John breathed.

"It was later that night after Betsy ate Lucy's head that she was killed. Think about it. If it had been Toby, he would have bragged about it at Aubrey's. Also, the Warden had said the blood from Besty was smeared all over the trailer as a message. I believe that message was from the twins because Betsy was yours, and they somehow blamed you for what happened to Lucy," Claire finished.

***

Earl and the twins sat quietly in Edith's room, watching her rest. She still hadn't woken up from the testing she went through earlier. Earl didn't care how long he had to wait to talk to Edith again as long as he got to. Just then, Dr. Halloway entered the room and quietly shut the door behind him.

"Sorry it took me so long to come and check on Edith, but it was a mess in the ER."

"That bad, uh?" asked Earl.

"Yes, apparently, three gentlemen picked a fight with the wrong person and paid dearly for it. In fact, we almost lost one of the gentlemen, but it looks like he will recover. He is now resting in a room around the corner," replied the doctor as he went about checking Edith's vitals. Earl had a sinking feeling he knew which three gentlemen had been brought in and who the wrong person they picked a fight with was.

"Was one of them named Toby?" asked Earl, already knowing the answer. Both of the twins were now again paying very close attention to the conversation at the mention of Toby.

"Why yes, he is the one that almost lost his life," replied the Doctor, surprised that Earl knew the patient. "Is he a friend of yours?"

"Not exactly," replied Earl dryly. "The gentleman that they picked a fight with, John Colt, is like a son to me. Believe me when I tell you that ALL three of those men that were brought in are lucky to be alive."

"Grandpa, we need to use the restroom," said Anabel all of a sudden.

"Huh? Oh, yes, of course, I will take you," Earl said as he started to rise out of the chair, but then Edith opened her eyes. Earl was immediately by her side, grabbing hold of her hand.

The Doctor also saw that Edith was awake and took out a small light that looked like a pen. He then shone the light in Edith's eyes, moving the light slowly from side to side. Edith's eyes would follow the light confirming that she was comprehensive of what was happening around her. Edith still couldn't talk, but the hand Earl was holding tightened around his own. Earl was so happy that he didn't even notice that Anna and Annabel had left the room.

Chapter 9
Wrong Place, Wrong Time

Toby kept slipping in and out of sleep. The painkillers the nurse had loaded him up with were starting to kick in. The surgeon had stopped the internal bleeding, and they had patched up his face the best they could. He still would need reconstructive surgery done, but they couldn't risk it at this time. The doctor said the reconstructive surgeries he would need would be long and hard, and Toby would have to heal from the internal damage first. They had told him he was lucky just to be alive, although he didn't feel that way at the moment. The pain he had gone through before the painkillers started kicking in had been overwhelming, and he didn't think he would make it through it.

"Click." The sound came from the one door to Toby's room. Toby tried to open his eyes fully to see what had caused the noise. However, one eye was swollen shut, and the other was heavy from the medication. The best he could do was open his one good eye halfway, but for only a few seconds at a time. So there he was, opening and closing his one good eye to try to see what had caused that clicking sound. When his eye was open, he could see the room was dark except for the monitors showing his vitals and that only lit up the area right around his head, chest, and some of his legs. Not seeing anything in the darkness, he wrote the noise off as a figment of his imagination. He started to drift off again when he heard the distinct shuffle of feet, followed by the whispers, "Lucy says he must be the one," came a voice. "Lisa agrees he must be the sacrifice," came another. Toby struggled hard to open his one good eye at the words, but it would barely open now.

"Lucy says the sacrifice is necessary to punish the other." came the first voice again.

"Yes, to punish the one that hurt Lucy, says Lisa," came the second voice.

Panicking, Toby was finally able to open his one eye enough, and he saw two pairs of eyes staring right back at him from the semi-darkness at the foot of his bed. Toby tried to scream, but his jaw had been wired shut. He tried to push the call button to call the nurse, but his hand wasn't obeying his commands, and just flopped around on the bed. Then to his horror, the eyes he had just seen were gone. All of a sudden, he felt something tighten around his neck and it started to cut into his skin. Toby wanted to get up. He wanted to cry out for help; he wanted so desperately to stop what could only be a nightmare produced from the medication that was given to him for the pain. But all he could do was lie there as whatever was around his neck cut through the skin and into his trachea. He could feel the blood running down his throat, and then he felt nothing.

***

Claire and John entered Edith's room to see Earl holding Edith's hand and the Doctor examining her.

"Claire, John, I am so glad you both are here to see this! The Doc says that Edith is aware of what's going on around her. The Doc here says that means there is a really good chance we are going to have Edith back again!" exclaimed Earl, barely containing his excitement.

"I did say there was a small possibility, but I don't want you to get too excited. The journey will be a very difficult one," claimed Doctor Hallaway, not wanting to have everyone get their hopes too high. He knew that although Edith did seem to be improving, the chance of her fully recovering just wasn't likely.

"Bah, you don't know my Edith. She is as strong a fighter as there ever was. She will win this battle, trust me!" Earl exclaimed proudly.

"Of course. I will let you folks catch up. I have my rounds to make," said Doctor Hallaway as he excused himself.

"Oh, I am so happy for the both of you!" exclaimed Claire after the doctor left the room. Then she came over and gave Earl a great big hug. After Claire let go of Earl, he went over to John and gave him a big hug in turn.

"I am so glad you are here, son! I thought for sure you would be in jail after the beating you gave Toby and his boys," said Earl as he let go of John.

"H-how did you know about T-toby?" John asked, confused because the only people that knew what had happened at Aubrey's and would have told Earl about the fight were standing in the room.

"The Doc mentioned three men were brought in earlier and that they were badly beaten. I knew Claire had left here in a hurry to stop you from going into town because she was told Toby was there. I put 2 and 2 together, then asked the Doc if one of the fellows' names was Toby which he said it was," replied Earl.

"T-toby is here?" John asked, surprised.

"Yeah, the Doc said he is in the room right around the corner." Replied Earl.

"Where are the twins?" asked Claire all of a sudden. With all of the excitement, she had forgotten the real reason she and John were here.

"Oh, God! I didn't even know they were gone, so excited I was about Edith! They said they needed to use the restroom. That's probably where they went," Earl said in a panic. Both Claire and John exchanged worried looks.

"I will go check on them," offered John, who then quickly left the room.

"I sure hope the girls are alright," Earl said, worried.

"I am sure John will find them and bring them back safely," Claire said as she offered Earl to sit down.

"Yeah, you're right," Earl said as he took a seat.

"Speaking of the twins, I found this picture of them and their parents at Aubrey's after the fight."

Claire sat down next to him as she pulled out the picture she had found and handed it to Earl. He took the picture and looked at it for a few moments without saying a word. Claire could see the moisture rim Earl's eyes as he looked upon his daughter Sarah. "Yes, this was the last photo they had taken together before Sarah's husband took his life," Earl told her, choking back the emotions.

"In the picture, the twins are holding their dolls, Lucy and Lisa. Yet, in the photos of twins that I remember seeing at your home, they didn't have the dolls," stated Claire.

"Yes, they didn't have the dolls until the summer before this photo. Sarah and her husband took the twins down to New Orleans for a vacation that year. They visited one of those tourist voodoo shops. The girls saw the dolls and instantly fell in love with them, so Sarah bought the dolls for the girls," replied Earl. Then, confused by the picture and the questions, Earl asked Claire, "what's all this about?"

***

As John went in search of the twins, alarms started going off from around the corner. As John rounded the corner, he saw the door to a room where the alarms were coming from slowly close shut. As John walked by the room, nurses and a doctor came rushing around the corner with medical equipment in tow. The nurses, pushing him out of the way, ran into the room. John didn't know why, but he looked in the room from the doorway to see what was happening. The doctor started calling out orders and then asked the nurse the patient's name. John heard the nurse say Toby Harnet, and his heart froze. Then one of the nurses screamed.

"Doctor, his throat!"

The doctor went over to look at what the nurse was talking about.

"Quick, get security! This man was murdered!" exclaimed the doctor, seeing that Toby's throat had been cut halfway through.

"Yes, doctor, right away!" exclaimed the first nurse as she ran out the room past John.

"Alright, no one touches anything until the police get here. Also, find out if anyone saw anyone recently leave this room," ordered the doctor.

"Him! We saw him outside the door when we came around the corner!" exclaimed another nurse who was now pointing directly at John, who was still standing there like an idiot with his mouth hanging wide open.

"N-no! It w-w-wasn't m-me!" exclaimed John, dumbfounded and not believing that this was actually happening.

"FREEZE!" Came a call from John's left. John turned around and saw two armed security guards with guns pointed directly at him.

***

Claire was about to answer Earl's question when an alarm could be heard going off around the corner from their room. Then there were voices and the sounds of something on wheels hurriedly being pushed down the hallway.

"The girls!" exclaimed Earl as he got up from his chair, meaning to go search for them himself. He didn't have to, however, because just then, the twins came into the room.

"Girls!" he exclaimed at the sight of them and then bent down and gave both of them a hug. "Why did you leave without me, and where did the two of you go?"

Claire was wondering the same thing, but before the twins could say anything, shouts for "security" and "call the police" could be heard coming from just outside the door.

"Where is John?" Claire asked the twins, starting to panic. "What did you two do!"

"Claire! What has gotten into you!" exclaimed Earl as he protectively pulled the twins closer to him after seeing Claire come out of her seat toward them. Claire stopped herself before she grabbed the children, who were now smiling at her. Instead of doing what she was going to do, she stormed out of the room to look for John.

As Claire came out of Edith's room, she saw nurses and patients being escorted down the hallway away from where the alarms were going off. Claire could hear shouts coming from around the corner. She could hear someone yelling for someone else to get on the ground with their hands in the air. Claire hurriedly came around the corner to see two security guards with their guns drawn and pointed directly at John, who stood there with his hands by his sides, clenching and unclenching.

"I said get down on the ground and keep your hands where we can see them!" yelled one of the security guards for the umpteenth time.

"We are gonna have to put him down," said the other security guard, low enough so the suspect wouldn't hear.

Claire, on the other hand, did hear what the security guard had said. She again looked at John and could see that the *Darkness* was coming and that the security guard was right. The *Darkness* would attack the guards, and they would have to open fire on John unless Claire quickly did something. Claire was still in her Sheriff's uniform and thought she had a way to calm everything down. All she needed to do was get the guards to lower their weapons and let her get close enough to John.

"Gentleman, what's going on here?" Claire asked in her most professional voice. One security guard, most likely the senior of the two guards, gave a quick glance at Claire. Seeing Claire's uniform slowly backed up to her without taking his sights off of John.

"This guy just killed a man in the room over there, and he is not complying with our demands," responded the guard. Claire tried hard to hide her shock. She knew that Toby was somewhere down this hall and John being here was too much of a coincidence. That means Toby was most likely the dead man.

"Oh, John! What trouble are you in now?" Claire asked under her breath. "What was that?" asked the security guard, not catching what Claire had said.

"Lower your guns. I will take it from here," Claire told the guard.

"Can't let you do it, ma'am. This man is a murderer and extremely dangerous," stated the guard.

"Let me?" snapped Claire. "I am a Sheriff, and I don't need your permission for anything. Now stand down while I talk to this man."

Both of the security guards looked at each other, and then the first one nodded to his partner. Both of the guards lowered their guns, but not all the way. Claire, thinking that this was going better than she had hoped, started slowly toward John. She stopped a short distance from him, and she could clearly see the struggle taking place.

"John, look at me," Claire said. There was no response. John just stood there with his fist clenching and unclenching. "Look at me!"

John looked at Claire, and the light came back to his eyes. Then all of a sudden, his eyes opened wide, and he started to convulse violently before falling to the ground. At first, Claire wasn't comprehending what was happening, and then she saw the wires coming out of John's back. She followed the wires from John's back to the stun gun one of the two police officers held in his hands. The second officer seeing John down, ran over, put a knee in the middle of John's back, and then handcuffed him. The two police officers must have come in from the back entrance, Claire thought. Then they must have waited to take John down when he was distracted.

"I am Sheriff Claire Davis, and this man is with me," Claire informed the first officer, the one that had shot John. The second officer rolled a handcuffed John onto his back.

"With all due respect, Sheriff, this man is believed to have just killed a patient here," replied Officer Miller, according to his name tag.

"With all due respect, this man didn't kill anyone?" Claire shot back while emphasizing the 'with all due respect.'

"Listen, we got a call that said a patient here had his throat cut halfway through, and this man was described standing outside the room right after the alarms went off," said Officer Miller, obviously annoyed by Claire's tone.

"So standing near a room when an alarm goes off is evidence of murder?" asked Claire, getting just as annoyed.

"Why was he standing there?" shot back Officer Miller, who obviously didn't like being put on the defensive.

Having been a city cop once, Claire knew that they didn't like county Sheriffs much. They thought of them as no more than glorified security guards. To top it off, Claire was willing to bet that this officer also didn't like being questioned by a woman.

"Mr. Colt here," Claire started, nodding toward a still prone John on the ground. "was looking for Mr. Claymore's twin daughters who had gone to use the restroom. Since the restrooms are down this same hall, it only stands to reason for Mr. Colt to be here."

"I didn't do it," said John.

"Shut up!" said the second officer, and he gave John a kick in the side.

"Kick him again, and it will be the last thing you do," stated Claire evenly. Both officers immediately turned to face Claire, and their eyes widened when they saw she had her hand resting on the hilt of her gun. They immediately put their hands to their weapons as well.

"Claire, what's going on?" came the question from the side of Claire. Claire glanced out of the corner of her eye while still keeping the officers in her sight to see Earl with the twins standing there looking confused and scared.

"Officer Miller, the gentleman standing there is Mr. Claymore, and the twin girls at his side are his granddaughters. They are also the girls that Mr. Colt was looking for when all the commotion happened, and they can testify to it," Claire said, indicating Earl and the girls. The entire time, though, she never took her eyes off the officers or her hand off her gun.

Officer Miller realized that there really wasn't much he could do to hold John, for there was no real evidence that John had done anything wrong except stand in a hallway. Officer Miller also knew, however, that he didn't want to get in a shootout with an obvious nut job of a Sheriff in the middle of a hospital. Still, he did receive a call that had to be investigated, and this man was the only possible suspect.

"Look, I don't want any problems. However, we still have to go by the protocol on this because there is a dead body, and he was the only one seen around the victim. I'll tell you what I will do. I will release him temporarily into your custody for now until a further investigation is done. But, you will take sole responsibility for him, deal?" offered Officer Miller, hoping that by offering the deal, it would bring the entire situation back to a reasonable level.

"Deal, now take the handcuffs off him and help him to his feet," responded Claire.

She took her hand off the hilt of her gun but did not change her stance.

The officer that had kicked John earlier took the cuffs off. Then both the officers helped him to his feet. John appeared to be able to stand on his own, although he twitched a few times here and there from the jolts of electricity he had suffered from the stun gun. He uneasily walked over to Claire, and the two officers left to mark off the crime scene and do their investigation.

"Will someone please tell me what the hell is going on!" Earl cried. "Claire?"

"I will have to update you later, Earl. Right now, I have to get John out of here before they do find something to hold him on," was all that Claire said. She then grabbed John and started down the hallway away from the crime scene.

Chapter 10
Claire Visits Detective Marshall

It was a long drive back to Claire's house. She didn't want to take John to his trailer because she knew he hadn't been home since Betsy's death.

Even though the Warden had said he had cleaned up John's trailer that night, Claire felt it might be too soon. So Claire decided to take John back to her place instead. John had slept the entire way to Claire's house. She had wanted to question him about what had happened at the hospital with Toby, but as soon as they had made it to the car, John was out cold. To top it off, she didn't get a chance to talk to Earl about the twins. The truth of the matter was, Claire herself was running on fumes the last couple of days and was just wanting the comfort of her own bed. The world would just have to wait another day for Claire to save it.

"John, wake up. We are home," Claire said, gently shaking him.

"Huh, where are we?" John asked, wiping the sleep away from his eyes.

The fact that John didn't react in a defensive manner at being shaken awake showed how drained he really was. Truth be told, the cumulation of all the crap that had happened in only a couple of days and, of course, being electrocuted tended to leave one exhausted.

"We are at my place. Come on, let's get you to bed." Replied Claire, getting out of the cruiser and coming around to his side of her car.

John was so tired he let Claire help him out of the car and lead him inside. She let John lean on her as she led him to the bedroom. Just as Claire went to ease John down onto the bed, Claire tripped over something, and they both landed in a heap on the ground. Together, they both yelped out in pain, then started laughing at the absurdity of it all. John pulled Claire close to him, and within seconds, both were sound asleep.

***

Earl woke up the next morning to the call of the rooster. He had brought the twins home from the hospital early yesterday. As soon as Claire had left with a stunned and shaky John, Earl felt it was best for him to leave with the girls right away. Earl didn't know what had happened in the hospital yesterday except that Toby had been murdered and somehow John had become a possible suspect. Earl didn't want to take the risk of being questioned by the police and possibly hurting John's case. So he slipped away with the girls before anyone could question him. Not that it would matter too much. At some point, the police were going to find out that it was John who had put Toby in the hospital in the first place. Once they did, they would have enough for probable cause to arrest him. To be honest, Earl was having a hard time trying to find John not guilty of murdering Toby. The only person that had even known that Toby was there at the hospital and would have had a grudge enough to see Toby dead was John. Maybe when John had met up with Toby at Aubrey's, he had gotten Toby to admit that he was the one that had killed Betsy. Maybe John had tried to kill Toby right then and there but wasn't able to finish the job. Maybe when

John had found out that Toby was there at the hospital, he saw his chance to finish that job. After all, John was surprised to hear Toby was in a room right around the corner and had been eager to volunteer to find the twins. *That's an awful lot of maybes,* thought Earl.

"No! John was a good lad and wouldn't have done it," Earl said aloud.

But, even though he said his thoughts out loud with conviction, there was a lingering doubt in the back of his mind.

Earl knew there wasn't much he could do about all the events that had happened yesterday at the moment. He just had to hope that John was innocent and that the real murderer would be caught soon. For now, Earl had to get out of bed and get the day started. He needed to get the breakfast made for the girls, and then he would get some much-needed work around the farm done before heading back to see Edith. A farm needs constant care, and with Earl being at the hospital all the time, a lot of the everyday chores had fallen way behind. After Earl had showered and shaved, he went downstairs to make breakfast for the twins.

However, when he entered the kitchen, the twins were already sitting at the table eating oatmeal. Both girls looked up at Earl and smiled.

"Good morning Grandpa!" both girls greeted Earl in unison. "We made you some breakfast," said Anna.

"We also made you your coffee," said Anabel.

"We made it just the way you like it," said Anna.

It took Earl a second to understand what the girls had said, for they both had spoken so fast, almost on top of each other. Earl had to admit that when the twins talked like that, it creeped him out a little. Earl noticed that at the end of the kitchen table, there was indeed a bowl of oatmeal and a cup of coffee. By the steam coming off the items, Earl guessed they were still hot. Again, Earl had to marvel at the change the girls had had since Edith had fallen down the stairs. They were now so eager to help out and were well behaved. Maybe once Edith came back home, everything would be fine after all, Earl thought. Earl sat down and started with a sip of his coffee. He was instantly hit with bitterness. He started to grimace but saw that both girls were watching him intently. Earl hid his original expression with a smile. Both girls, seeing him smile, seemed pleased by his reaction. The rest of breakfast went off without a hitch, and then the girls asked Earl if they could play in the field out back while he attended to his daily chores. Earl let them go play and then got up to put away the dishes. As he got up from the table, he noticed two sets of small dirt tracks across the kitchen floor.

"When did the girls bring that in?" asked Earl out loud; then, shrugging it off, he went about cleaning it up.

***

Claire awoke to the sun shining brightly through the bedroom window. Yawning, she looked around and was surprised that she was in her bed. John must have put me here at some point, she thought to herself. After a few stretches and some convincing, Claire finally got out of bed. That's when she also noticed that she was completely naked. John must have also removed her uniform. The thought of him doing so instantly brought a mischievous smile to her face. Claire jumped in the shower, then got dressed in one of her clean uniforms. She then went downstairs, hoping to find John cooking her breakfast just like in a romance novel, but the house was completely empty.

"I guess breakfast was too much to ask for," Claire grumbled out loud. She did find a note on the kitchen table from John letting her know that he had taken her other car, not the police cruiser, to go home and would be back later. Sighing, Claire made her breakfast and headed to work.

When Claire arrived at the Station, Deputy Jones was already there. He didn't say anything, only just stared hard at Claire. Not knowing what his problem was and not really caring, Claire went to her desk. She started going through her papers when finally Travis got up and walked over to stand in front of her desk. He didn't say anything, just stood there staring at her.

"Do you need something, Deputy?" Claire asked, stopping what she was doing to stare right back at Travis.

"You let that bastard go!" Travis exclaimed.

"What bastard would that be?" asked Claire, her eyes narrowing.

"Your boyfriend, that's who!" yelled Travis. Claire came forward in her chair and stared right back at Travis with the same intensity he was giving.

"Mr. Colt was let go because the witnesses at the diner verified that he had acted in self-defense," explained Claire with a calm and steady voice.

"And what about Toby being killed last night at the hospital? The same hospital that you and John just happened to be at!" accused Travis. Seeing Claire's expression change to surprise at him knowing about Toby's death only provoked Travis more. "That's right. I know all about it. Dale called me and told me all about it last night. By your expression, I am guessing you forgot that both Jake and Dale were still being treated at the hospital when Toby was murdered.

Claire did totally forget that the two had been taken to the hospital. She had been so caught up in finding the photo at Aubrey's that all she had been focused on was the twins. How stupid of her, she thought. Of course, they were taken to the same hospital. It was the only real hospital around for miles. Damn! That meant they would have most likely told Officer Miller that it was John that had put them and Toby there. Now they would have probable cause to arrest John. As if reading her mind, Claire saw a smile spread across Deputy Jones' face.

"What?" Claire asked, already tired of this game.

"An Officer Miller from the St. Louis Police department called and said you have 24 hours to bring your boyfriend in for questioning. He said if you don't, not only will they come to arrest him, but you will be arrested as well for aiding and abetting," answered Travis with a smile that only grew bigger at Claire's obvious discomfort.

Claire wanted nothing more than to knock that smug smile right off Travis's face, and she almost did. However, right as she was building up to take the swing, the phone began to ring. Not taking her eyes off Travis, Claire picked up the phone.

"Hello," Claire greeted.

"Tick-tock, tick-tock," whispered Travis while tapping his watch with his finger. Claire shot him a look that said she was done with him, and the Deputy just turned around and left the station house laughing in response.

"Yes, this is Sheriff Davis," answered Claire. The speaker on the other end told Claire that Detective Marshall would be in his office today and that he had what Claire had requested. "Yes, I will be there in a couple of hours. Thank you so much."

Claire hung up the phone and grabbed her gear as she had to drive to St. Louis to see Detective Marshall. If her hunch was right, she would have enough compelling evidence to keep John and herself from getting arrested.

"Crap!" Claire exclaimed. "John doesn't know that he is about to be taken in. Sallie Mae, please get a hold of Mr. Colt and let him know that he might be having some unwanted guests stopping by. Tell him to stay safe until I can get back to him."

"You got it, honey!" replied Sallie Mae as she immediately started the call to reach John. Claire was already gone before Sallie Mae even finished the word, honey.

***

Deputy Jones sped down the roadway away from the Sheriff's station.

Coming fast to the intersection where the roadway met the highway, the Deputy made a hard right onto the highway without slowing. Luckily for the Deputy, there had been no other vehicles coming down the highway, for if there had been, there would have definitely been a collision.

"Fuck that Bitch!" cursed the Deputy out loud while pounding one of his fists on the dashboard.

"Who does that bitch think she is? First, she sweeps into town, taking the position of Sheriff, a position that was supposed to be mine by rights. Then she had to go make lovey-dovey with that freak of a retard military hero. Next, she had the nerve to punch me in my nose for making a little harmless joke. Now, she is going to help that retard murderer walk free," the Deputy ranted out loud.

"Well, you know what? That shit isn't going to happen on my watch."

The Deputy slammed on the breaks spinning the cruiser around, and started heading back in the direction he had just come from. A few minutes later, he came to a side road he had just passed and took a turn. After about a twenty-minute drive, he pulled up to a very nice plantation house. The house was two stories with a lot of picture windows lining it. The house was painted in light green, with the framework and pillars painted white. The front porch was the entire length of the front of the house. It was probably the nicest house in the entire town, and it belonged to Jake Nickels. Deputy Jones got out of his cruiser and stormed up the porch to the front door, where he pounded on the door feverishly.

"Knock it off! I'm coming. Just wait a damn minute!" yelled a voice from inside. A few moments later, Jake opened the door.

"Damn!" Exclaimed Deputy Jones. It was the first time he had gotten to see Jake in person, and in the sunlight, it definitely wasn't pretty. Jake's nose had been broken, and thus, it was still bandaged. Jake's eyes were still swollen, with black and blue marks outlining them. "You look like shit!"

"Fuck you, man! I don't need this shit!" yelled Jake, who proceeded to close the front door on the Deputy. Jake had gotten home earlier that morning, and even though he was loaded up with painkillers, he had just gotten to sleep. So he really wasn't in the mood to entertain any guest, especially a rude one. Deputy Jones was quicker, though, and stopped the door from being shut with an outstretched hand.

"Alright, alright. I am sorry, it just caught me off guard, is all," Travis said in a much gentler tone. If he was going to do what he needed to do, he would need both Jake and Dale to pull it off. "Listen, I came by because that soldier boy that did that to your face has a warrant out on him, and I want to be the one that serves it to him. But, I am going to need your and Dale's help."

"You are out of your fucking mind, man! I ain't going anywhere near that freak, period! I am not going to risk my ass just so you can take that nut job to prison," retorted Jake, who again tried to close the door, but Deputy Jones was the stronger and easily held Jake's attempts off.

"We are not going to be taking him to jail. The warrant just says he needs to be brought in," said the Deputy, saying the last sentence slowly. Deputy Jones didn't know exactly how much medication Jake was on, but he wanted Jake to fully understand his full intention on the subject. "The warrant just says he needs to be brought in. It doesn't say anything about him being alive."

Jake didn't know if it was the drugs he had recently popped or possibly the swelling in his brain, but the sound of the retard being killed did sit very well with him at that moment. The idea must have shown on his face, for Deputy Jones smiled and let go of the door.

"Listen, get some sleep, then get Dale and meet me 5 miles down the road from the retard's property at dusk. I will bring all the firepower we need, and we will go in after dark," said the Deputy with a gleam in his eyes. He then turned to walk away.

For a moment, Jake almost called out to the Deputy to stop him. He did want the retard dead, but he did not want to die in the process. A wave of pain rolled through his head, reminding him of what John had done to him.

"Get the guns and let's bury that fucker," said Jake out loud, then he shut the door.

***

It was well into the afternoon before Earl got all his chores done, which happened to be a lot. His knees and back hurt very badly by the end of it. So much so that he had a hard time getting back up from clearing the brush around the water well. For the second time, he wondered how he was going to manage it all. Raising the twins and taking care of Edith and the farm was simply too much for an old man whose body just wasn't up to handling the load. He was definitely going to have help if he was going to try and pull it all off. He knew he could count on John to help, that was if he didn't end up in prison. There was also Claire, that would offer assistance, again, if she didn't end up in prison herself. No, he would probably have to hire someone, but with what money. Shaking his head at the insanity of it all, he dusted off his pants and headed inside to get the girls for a picnic trip.

Earl entered the house to find both girls sitting on the couch with a picnic basket, all ready to go. Earl smiled at the sight of them, and he then knew he had to try to make it all work.

"Well, aren't the two of you just eager beavers? You both really want to go on that picnic very badly," said Earl, smiling as their faces lit up.

"Yes, Grandpa," replied Anna.

"Yes, we are eager beavers just like you said," chimed in Anabel.

"Lisa and Lucy are also very excited," said Anna, picking up pace.

"We can't wait to make you happy," said Anabel, matching her sister's speed.

"Yes, once you are in the garden, we will make you happy," said Anna.

"Yes, happy forever." finished Anabel.

It took Earl a second to decipher what the twins had said, but he decided that he was too tired. All he knew was that they were eager to get to the garden and make him happy.

"Well, alright then. Let me go wash up, and we will be off." Earl told them and started to head up the stairs to clean up. The twins, however, had a different plan. They each grabbed Earl by his arms and started dragging him to the door.

"We must go now, Grandpa," said Anna.

"Yes, you will ruin the surprise," said Anabel.

Earl did not understand the twins' eagerness or what the surprise Anabel mentioned was, but it was getting late in the day. If they wanted to get to the garden and have a picnic, they would have to leave now. So Earl grabbed the picnic basket and headed out the door with twins and their dolls in tow.

It was an extremely beautiful day outside. The sky was a beautiful blue fill with cotton ball clouds spread all about. The sun was already heading toward the horizon since it was well past noon. There was a gentle breeze that kept the summer heat at bay. As Earl walked, the girls ran around him with their dolls in the air as if they all were flying. Earl continually found himself smiling and laughing at the sight of the girls enjoying life. As they approached where the garden was, Earl found himself smiling again, but not because of the girls. No, he was smiling because he knew as soon as he made his way through the brush, he would look upon Edith's garden and know she was there with them in spirit, if not in person.

"My God! What!" exclaimed Earl, who was now no longer smiling, for when he came through the brush, he didn't just see Edith's beautiful garden. He saw that part of the garden had been dug up. Where there once had been rows of beautiful tulips, there was now a hole that looked like a shallow grave. Earl dropped the picnic basket and stumbled to the edge of the hole. Completely stunned by what he was seeing, could only get the words out. "Who would have done such a thing!"

***

Claire arrived at the St. Louis police department at about 1 p.m. and immediately went to find the Detective Marshal's office. She wanted to get in and out of there as fast as possible before someone recognized her. However, it was probably pointless since she was still in her Sheriff's uniform and stuck out like a sore thumb. After checking a directory, she found that the Detective Marshal's office was off to the left wing on the first floor. This was good for Claire because she could get there from the outside with very little to no interactions. After about ten minutes, Claire finally arrived at the Detectives Marshal's office. Claire straightened her uniform before knocking on the door.

"Come in," a man's voice came from within after Claire knocked.

Claire turned the doorknob and entered the office. It was a very plain and non-descript-looking room. The walls were bare, with no pictures or decorations of any kind. The carpet was dull grey or brown. Claire couldn't tell, for it was very soiled. The carpet was also heavily worn in spots indicating someone spending a lot of time pacing back and forth. There were a couple of filing cabinets along the wall. The drawers were half open and the files inside were strewn. There was a large wooden desk in the middle of the room with papers thrown about on top of it. There were only two chairs in the room, one in front of the desk and one behind the desk, which was now occupied by a very large man.

"You must be Detective Marshall," Claire stated as she approached the desk and extended her hand in a formal greeting.

"And you must be Sheriff Davis," replied Detective Marshall as he stood up to shake her offered hand and then offered her a seat in the empty chair across from him. After they were both seated, the Detective continued. "Sheriff Davis, I have to admit I was surprised to have received a message that you wanted to see the autopsy records of Mrs. Sarah Brown's dead husband, Neil Brown."

"Why is that?" Asked Claire.

"Well, for one, the way Sarah Brown had died just didn't add up for me, especially the way it had been written off. Then you come along and start asking questions about the husband's death which got me thinking maybe I had missed something," replied the Detective taking out a cigarette and lighting it. He offered Sarah one, but she respectfully declined.

"How exactly was Sarah's death written off?" asked Claire.

"Officially, the file says that basically Sarah's drugged-up boyfriend, Mr. Johnson, had forced her to overdose on prescription drugs. Then Mr. Johnson, in turn, overdosed on the same drugs," replied the Detective.

"But you don't believe that, do you?" asked Claire, coming a little forward in her chair.

"Let's just say I found the way she had died a little disturbing," replied the detective, who was now paying very close attention to Claire.

"Disturbing? How so?" asked Claire leaning even more forward in her Chair.

"There were a few things that didn't make sense when I arrived at the scene. First, I was told that the victim, Mrs. Brown, had overdosed on prescription drugs which were supposedly forced down her by her boyfriend, Mr. Johnson. Yet, I did not see any signs of a struggle in the apartment or on her body."

"Who had said that the drugs were forced down her by her boyfriend?" interrupted Claire.

"The 911 call was made by one of her twin daughters, Anna, I think. Yes, Anna, and she had said on the call that Mr. Johnson had forced her mother to take the pills," replied the Detective, noticing that Claire was taking a strong interest in everything he was saying.

"Please continue," offered Claire.

"However, the M.E on the scene pointed out there were no signs of abuse on her body, not even any defense wounds, that would indicate struggle against being force-fed. In fact, there were no marks of any kind on her body that would normally be associated with one being physically attacked. None, at least not until you got to her ankles." The Detective paused here, noticing that Claire started to shake at the mention of the ankles. Finding this very peculiar, the Detective continued, "There, on her ankles, we had discovered thin lines with dry blood spots caked on both her ankles as if she had been bound with something."

Claire suddenly came flying fully forward in her seat, planting her hands on the desk. The Detective, completely taken by surprise by Claire's intense reaction, carefully backed his chair away from his desk and Claire. Claire, seeing the Detective move away from her cautiously, made her calm down and regain control of her emotions.

"I apologize for my behavior. It's just that I am very invested in this case. Sarah Brown used to be Sarah Claymore, the daughter of friends of mine," apologized Claire, and she calmly sat back down again.

"That's alright. I understand how the job can get to someone. I have been there myself from time to time," replied the detective, slowly pulling his chair back up to his desk. "However, that was a pretty big reaction over me discovering a couple of marks on Mrs. Brown's ankles."

"Yes, of course. It is just that I had also noticed the same lines on Sarah's ankles at her funeral. Since then, I have seen similar marks three times after that. One was on the neck of a butchered pig, a second one on the neck of a town bully who was murdered last night, a murder which is now being pinned on a friend of mine, finally, the third was on Mrs. Claymore, Sarah's mother, who now is lying in a hospital bed paralyzed from the neck down after supposedly falling down the stairs. All three victims can be tied back to Sarah and her family," replied Claire, who made sure to emphasize the word family. Now it was her turn to watch the Detective's reaction.

Detective Marshall's cigarette had fallen out of his hand and landed on the desk. His mouth hung open, and Claire knew that the detective was starting to put the pieces together.

"That's why you asked about the husband," replied the detective picking his cigarette back up.

"Yes. A friend of the Claymores told me that Sarah had come home and found her husband in the garage sitting in the car, dead. That it was ruled as a suicide," replied Claire.

"Yes, they ruled it a suicide by carbon monoxide poisoning," confirmed the detective.

"But, you never really looked at the autopsy report, did you?" accused Claire.

"To be honest, the coroner ruled it as a suicide, so I didn't feel the need to. I get several cases a day, so if the coroner rules it a suicide, I have to move on to the next case," replied the Detective defensively.

Claire wasn't surprised, St. Louis had a very high murder rate, and unfortunately, a lot of cases got lost, buried, or ignored. Especially suicide cases.

"But, you did get the report for me at my request?" Claire pushed.

"Yes, it was sent over just this morning," replied the Detective, grabbing a sealed manila envelope from the desk drawer and tossing it to Claire.

Claire eagerly grabbed the envelope and opened it, dumping the contents on the desk. It was definitely the autopsy report, and after only a few moments of reading, Claire stood straight up as she found exactly what she was looking for.

She slammed the papers down in front of the Detective and pointed at the paragraph she had just read. The Detective leaned forward and read what she was pointed at.

"Well, I'll be damned!" exclaimed the detective.

"Sarah's husband had the same marks on his neck as she had on her ankles," Claire said triumphantly as she gave the Detective a disgusted look at his incompetence.

"The coroner probably thought Mr. Brown had probably tried to kill himself before, maybe by trying to hang himself. When he did not succeed, the coroner probably figured Mr. Brown had moved on to the carbon monoxide route," said the Detective more to himself than to Claire. "But, who?"

"Anna and Anabel!" Claire shouted, frustrated at the detective's continued ignorance.

"The twin daughters?" asked the detective, astonished.

"Think about it. When the dad was found, where were the girls?" Claire asked.

"According to the report, they were both playing in the front yard," replied the Detective.

"Both girls were just casually playing in the front yard, unsupervised, while the dad offs himself in the garage?" Claire asked, trying to draw a picture for the detective. "What were the girls doing when the police showed up at Sarah's house the night she had died?"

"The cops who reached the scene first reported that both girls were just sitting in the living room playing with their dolls," replied the detective in a whisper as he remembered that night talking with Detective Jenkins and how he had mentioned the girl's behavior was weird.

"So the girls were right there at both parents' deaths, acting casual like there was no care in the world, and you didn't find that unusual? You didn't think to find a connection? You should have checked! You also should have done a better job searching the crime scene! I am willing to bet that if you did, you would have found the fishing line the twins had used on their parents that had caused those marks!" shouted Claire.

Noticing that the Detective all of a sudden turned a shade whiter, Claire asked, "What?"

"When CSI turned in their findings, they did mention that all they could find was some fishing line in the mother's sewing kit." gasped the Detective, now realizing it was there all along. Claire didn't think the Detective could turn in whiter, but he did as he suddenly thought of something else.

"What is it, now?" Claire asked, almost scared to hear the answer.

"Ron Johnson," gasped the Detective.

"He is still alive?" asked Claire.

"He hung himself two days ago. After his overdose, he still lived. We tried to interview him, but his mind was too far gone, so they threw him in a mental hospital. They never could get anything out of him. All he would do is repeat the same phrase over and over again," said the Detective.

"What was the phrase?" asked Claire, truly shaken now.

"Lisa and Lucy want to play. Lisa and Lucy will make you pay," whispered the Detective.

***

Earl stumbled forward from the first blow to the back of the head, and then he was hit in the knees, followed by another blow to the back of the head again. An explosion of pain seared through his head and knees. No longer being able to keep his balance with the pain caused by the repeated blows, Earl found himself falling forward into the freshly dug hole. Somehow as Earl fell, his body twisted on the way down so that he landed hard on his back while facing the sky. He looked up to see both Anna and Anabel standing at the lip of the hole above him, both with shovels in their hands. Earl tried to get up, but his knee was badly hurt, and the searing pain in his head only made him want to vomit.

He moved his hand to the back of his head and found it soaked with blood. Then a shovel full of dirt landed on his chest. Earl looked back up at the twins just as another shovel full of dirt hit him square in the face. He tried to wipe the dirt from his face, but another pile of dirt hit him again. Earl tried desperately to get up, but as he managed to get himself propped up on one elbow, a rock hit him square in the temple, knocking him back to the ground.

"No, you don't, Grandpa, you have to stay still," said Anna, the one who had thrown the rock.

"You must not ruin the surprise," said Anabel, who chucked another pile of dirt onto Earl's face.

"You must stay still," repeated Anna.

"You must let us send you to Mommy and Daddy," said Anabel.

"So we can all be happy together again, just like Grandma told us," said Anna.

Earl could barely hear the last thing Anna had said because the dirt completely covered his head now. He tried to breathe but only sucked in the dirt. A little while later, Anna and Anabel, swinging Lisa and Lucy in the air between them, made their way back home.

Chapter 11
Lisa and Lucy Want to Play

John's natural instinct was to run even though he was innocent. He was trained to be a survivor at any cost, and he wouldn't spend the rest of his life in prison. So after John got off the radio with Sallie Mae, he had decided the best thing for him to do was disappear. He had gathered all the things he needed to take with him, which was mostly camping and hunting gear. He buried some personal items he couldn't take with him in the woods. He hoped someday he would be able to come back and collect them. The sun was setting, and dusk was starting to take over by the time he had all the tasks that needed to be done finalized. He took a final look at the trailer that had been his home and started off into the woods on foot.

***

Deputy Jones paced back and forth impatiently in front of his squad car. The adrenaline had been pumping strongly through him all day for the thought of what he was about to do, so he had arrived at the designated meeting place early. However, it was now half-past the designated time, and there was still no sign of Jake and Dale. Now, the adrenaline was mixed with fear that he would have to do this all alone.

"Fuck you, you assholes!" screamed the Deputy to no one. Storming to the back of his vehicle, he popped the trunk and grabbed his assault rifle and a duffle bag. The duffle bag was loaded with extra rifle mags loaded up with ammo, tear gas canisters, a tear gas launcher, and smoke grenades. Slamming the trunk down hard, he slung the rifle over one shoulder and the duffle bag over the other. He was about to take off into the woods in the direction of John's trailer when he heard a vehicle approaching. Turning around, he saw that it was Jake's Shelby Mustang. He set his gear back down as the car came to a stop behind his Cruiser.

"Sorry we are late, but Dale needed some convincing," Jake offered as he got out of his car and saw the hostility on the Deputy's face. Dale didn't get out of the car and actually shrunk down further back in his seat as Travis turned his glare toward him. Travis picked up his rifle again, but he didn't sling it over his shoulder this time.

"Do you still need convincing, Dale?" asked Travis as he raised his rifle and pointed it directly at Dale. Dale's eyes popped wide open, and he shook his head vigorously. "Good, then get the fuck out of the car and let's go!"

Dale quickly jumped out of the car and sheepishly joined Jake at the Deputy's trunk. Travis once again opened his trunk, where he grabbed another rifle, this one a hunting rifle with a scope, and handed it to Jake. Then he reached back in the trunk and pulled out a shotgun that he tossed to Dale. Dale, who obviously did not want to be there and wasn't expecting the throw, flinched reflexively. So instead of catching the incoming shotgun, he fumbled it, and the shotgun smacked him in his already bruised face, then it fell to the ground. Dale let out a yelp and then looked sheepishly at the ground. Travis just looked at him angrily and shook his head before storming off. Jake bent down, picked up the fallen shotgun, and then handed it to Dale sympathetically. Then they both were rushed to catch up with the Deputy, who was already moving quickly into the woods.

It was already dark by the time the trio finally got to their destination. Their destination was a little ways back in the woods, where they could barely make out John's trailer in the moonlight. Travis indicated a tree to Jake a little ways off that had somewhat of a perch that Jake would be able to snipe from. Jake nodded, knowing he was both the sniper and the lookout for the team. He moved quickly toward the spot. Travis then motioned to Dale to get to John's truck. Dale was to make sure that if John got out of the trailer and tried to escape that he wouldn't be able to drive away. At first, Dale didn't move, he just stood there with a pleading look on his face, but Travis smacked him hard across the head, dropping him to the ground. He then picked Dale back up by his collar and gave him a rough shove in the direction of John's truck. Finally, Travis went off in the opposite direction of Jake and Dale. He was going around to the other side of the trailer. He was to flush John out so that either Jake or Dale could take him down. Once Travis found his spot, he dropped the duffle bag and opened it up. He pulled out the tear gas launcher and loaded it up. He was to wait ten minutes to give Jake and Dale enough time to get in position.

***

"Sallie Mae, this is the Sheriff. Are you there, over?" asked Claire over her car radio. Claire was flying down the highway with her lights flashing and her siren blaring. She didn't know how, but she had a sinking feeling that if she didn't get to Earl, something bad was going to happen to him.

"I'm here, Sheriff, over," came Sallie Mae's voice over the radio.

"Listen, I need you to try to call the Claymore's residence and get ahold of Mr. Claymore. It's an emergency, over," Claire said with apparent urgency. The silence while Claire waited was overwhelming.

"Sorry Sheriff, no one is responding, over," came the reply over the radio.

"Try the hospital, over," responded Claire desperately. Ten long minutes passed before Sallie Mae responded.

"Sorry, Sheriff, they said that Mr. Claymore never showed up for a visit today. Over."

"Listen, try to get a hold of John. If he doesn't answer, I want you to keep saying this over his radio loud and clear: 'It was the twins. Meet me, Claire, at the Claymores' repeatedly for the next 30 minutes. I am headed over the Claymores right now, over," instructed Claire. Not waiting for an answer, Claire pushed the gas pedal all the way to the floor. All she could do was hope she could get to the Claymores in time before something bad happened. She prayed her gut was wrong and that when she showed up, Earl would be alright, but she couldn't help feeling her gut was right.

***

John squatted down in a bush not far from his trailer. He had made it a couple of miles before the more rational side took over. He couldn't run from his problems while leaving Earl and Edith behind, not when they needed him the most. He knew he was innocent, and so did Claire, which was the other reason he had decided not to run away.

Claire had become his whole world. He would never leave her side. So, after he had made his decision, he turned around and came back home to wait for a word from Claire. However, as he had gotten close to his trailer, his survival instincts came to the fore, and he felt something was very wrong. He didn't know exactly what it was, but it made him pick a hiding space that would give him the best advantage over his surroundings. Even though it was dark, the moon lit up his trailer and the area around it enough for John to see if there was a threat. He had been holding his position when he heard Sallie Mae's voice come in over his radio which he had left in his trailer.

"John, this Sallie Mae. If you can hear me, Claire says it's the twins and to meet her over at the Claymores, over."

After hearing Sallie Mae's message and the urgency in the voice, John started to get up and go to his trailer to reply. That's when all hell broke loose. Shots rang out into the night, and bullets riddled John's trailer. John instinctively dropped to the ground behind some deadwood. He knew an assault rifle firing when he heard one and knew the owner was well equipped. The firing went on as holes were driven through John's trailer, destroying anything and everything that was inside. John knew if he wanted to get to Claire, he would have to deal with this. Flipping the switch, John allowed the *Darkness* to take over. As the gunfire stopped, most likely due to the owner changing mags to reload, the *Darkness* sped off to hunt.

***

Deputy Jones hadn't meant to start shooting just yet. He had hoped to scout out the place first to make sure that John was in his trailer. However, when he had heard the sound of Sallie Mae's voice, the adrenaline and fear took over, causing him to react before he intended to. Well, there's no use dwelling on it now. What's done was done.

The Deputy thought to himself. He just had to hope John had been sleeping and that some of the bullets he just rained down on the trailer had found their mark. Putting the rifle down, he quickly picked up the tear gas launcher. Making sure his aim was true, he sent canister after canister into the windows of the trailer.

***

Dale had been hiding on the side of John's truck that was facing the woods. He had a perfect view of the trailer door from his position. If John came out, Dale would have an excellent shot. This did little to calm Dale's nerves, though, which showed as his body shook uncontrollably and his hands became sweaty. Both of these issues would most likely make his chances of actually hitting John nearly impossible, even being close to the target. Dale heard Sallie Mae's voice come over the radio and the message she was apparently trying to deliver. It was something about it being the twins, but Dale had no idea what that meant. Then all of a sudden, gunfire rang out into the night, scaring poor Dale so much that he dropped the shotgun on the ground. He, too, instinctively dropped down to the ground, where he grabbed the shotgun and scrambled his way back to the truck for cover. What the hell was going on, thought Dale. Travis was supposed to get eyes on the target first and then use tear gas to flush John out. Why in the hell was he shooting at the trailer? Unless John knew they were there and took the Deputy by surprise. Now that was truly a scary thought.

"Fuck this, I'm out!" exclaimed Dale. He made a mad dash for the cover of the woods. He was almost to the tree line before something heavy suddenly hit him in the back, propelling him forward and causing him to fall to the ground face first. Dale, in a panic, tried to frantically get up. However, when he tried to push himself up off the ground, he found he had no strength, and worse, he couldn't breathe! He opened his mouth to gasp for air, but instead, blood poured out. Then Dale felt someone heavy step on his back, keeping him pinned to the ground. He did manage to turn his head to the side enough to see in the moonlight that it was John who had one foot on his back holding him down. He watched in horror as John reached down and tugged on something that was stuck in his back. Dale felt a sharp pain as John slipped the object free. Dale's eyes widened for an instant as he recognized the object was a large knife with blood dripping from it, his blood! Then Dale knew no more.

***

Jake, sitting on his perch in a tree some distance from the trailer, didn't hear Sallie Mae's message come over the radio. So, when the shots rang out into the night and bullets started ripping through the trailer, he nearly fell out of the tree.

"What the hell is Travis doing?" Jake whispered to himself as he once again settled himself securely back in position. Like Dale, Jake knew this wasn't part of the plan they had discussed and that something definitely went wrong. The only thing Jake could think of was that John somehow had figured out what they were up to and set a trap himself. This last thought did not sit well at all with Jake either. In fact, he started having the same thought process that Dale had. Sure at first, Jake had been all in when Travis had shown up talking about making John pay. But, as time went on and remembering the beating John had recently given him made him start to rethink the whole idea. In fact, he was going to say something to Travis back there on the road. However, when Jake had seen Travis point the rifle at poor Dale, he wisely kept his mouth shut.

The shooting had suddenly stopped, then came the tear gas canisters. Too late to run now Jake thought as he lifted his rifle back up and looked down the scope. He could barely see the front of John's trailer through all the tear gas coming out of the now busted windows. Jake sat there, rifle ready, for John to come running out, but after several long moments, the tear gas started to dissipate with no sight of John. *Did Travis get lucky and hit John with one of the many bullets that had ripped through the trailer?* Jake thought to himself.

Suddenly Jake felt something sharp cut his throat right open. He dropped his rifle and grabbed his throat with both hands. He could feel his life's blood squirt through his fingers, and then he was falling, hitting branches on his way down. Jake's body hit the ground hard, but it didn't matter, for he no longer felt pain. He no longer felt anything.

***

Travis had used all six of his tear gas canisters, figuring overkill was probably a good idea. Always better to be safe than sorry, he thought. He was confident that with all the tear gas and bullets he had sent into the trailer, it was enough to take out anyone or anything that was inside. If John was inside the trailer, he was either dead or soon would be. Travis grabbed his rifle and started to make his way around the trailer to where he had sent Jake and Dale. While he made his way, he made sure to keep one eye on the trailer for any movement. Little did he know, he should have been keeping both eyes on where he was stepping, for he tripped over something and landed on his side in something wet. Travis hurried back to his feet and wiped away some of the muck from his face. But, when he brought his hand away from his face, he could see in the moonlight that his hand was covered in blood, not muck. Travis quickly looked back at what he had tripped over, and in the moon's glow, he could see that it was Jake's body. In a panic, Travis grabbed his assault rifle and tried to look all around him at once. Under other circumstances, an outside viewer would have found it comical. Travis, not seeing anything, started making his way to John's truck to get Dale. A few moments later, Travis found Dale just as he had found Jake: dead. Travis knew that he should turn and run, that if he stayed, he was going to soon end up like Jake and Dale.

"No! I won't let you beat me!" screamed Travis for all to hear. He grabbed his rifle and started randomly shooting in all directions. After Travis emptied the first magazine into the night, he quickly reloaded his last magazine and continued firing. After Travis ran through his last magazine, he just stood there pulling the trigger, but now all the rifle did was make a clicking sound. Then, out of the darkness in front of him, John walked toward him. Travis panicked at first, seeing this ghostly specter that somehow didn't even seem human in the moonlight coming toward him, but then he noticed the two bullet wounds leaking blood from John's abdomen.

"I got you!" Travis shouted to the specter. *I shot him! This isn't some ungodly demon! This was just a simple retard that bleeds, and that means he can die!* All these thoughts quickly ran through Travis's mind, especially the last one. Seeing John wounded had put some bravery back into Travis, and he waved John to come on. But then John suddenly stopped about fifteen feet from him. His arm moved extremely fast, too fast for Travis to comprehend, and Travis felt something hit him hard, square in the chest. Looking down, Travis saw the hilt of a knife sticking out of him. He looked back up at John with disbelief on his face, but John was already fading back into the shadows.

***

As Claire drove up the driveway of the Claymore house, she noticed that no lights were turned on inside. She had checked in one more time with Sallie Mae to see if she had gotten ahold of either Earl or John and had been told that both of them were unreachable, as was Travis. When Claire had questioned why Sallie

Mae was looking for Travis, she told Claire that it was because of what Mary Beth had told Sallie Mae earlier.

Mary Beth had heard a rumor that Jake and Dale were going to meet Travis at John's trailer for payback. When Claire heard this, she almost went to John's trailer instead of the Claymores'. Her gut, however, told her that checking on Earl was a higher priority. Besides, John could handle himself. Claire just had to hope that John had somehow heard Sallie Mae relaying her message over the radio and was now on his way to meet her there. She pulled her cruiser to a stop right in front of the house with her headlamps lighting up the front porch. She waited to see if her lights shining in the windows would spark some kind of reaction from inside, but there was no sign that anyone was home. Claire slowly got out of her cruiser and took a quick look around, hoping to see John coming out of the darkness to go with her inside the house. But there was nothing, just an eerie silence. She didn't have to go into the house. She could just leave and wait until tomorrow, then come back in the daylight. Maybe she was wrong in coming here and not going to John first, she thought to herself.

"No! I made the right decision. I have to go in," Claire accidentally said out loud. She jumped at the sound of her own voice, which the eerie silence had seemed to only amplify. Taking one last deep, steadying breath, Claire slowly approached the front porch. As she started to climb the porch stairs, the front door slowly swung open while making a loud creaking noise. Claire felt her bladder give away as droplets of urine soiled her pants. Strengthening her resolve and gritting her teeth, she held up her gun and pointed it toward the now open doorway. Mustering what little courage she could, she entered the Claymores' house. The light from her cruiser's headlamps only reached a little way into the foyer, casting scary-looking shadows along the ceiling and walls.

"Earl! It's Claire. Are you in here?" Claire shouted into the darkness. Hearing no response, she pulled out her flashlight and proceeded to clear the living room.

She didn't find anything out of place in the living room and started toward the kitchen when she suddenly heard giggling coming from upstairs. She immediately turned toward the giggling sounds and waited, trying to determine which direction they had come from, but now there was only silence again. She approached the stairs and shined her light up them with her gun still drawn. Claire slowly began to climb the stairs. Wincing every time one of the wooden steps groaned under her weight. As Claire reached the last step before stepping fully into the hallway, she paused to steady herself.

Then Claire came up the last step and around the corner, shining her light and gun down the hallway in a rush. She had expected the twins to be standing there looking all macabre, like something out of a horror flick ready to kill her. Instead, all she saw was an empty hallway.

"Claire," came the call from somewhere downstairs.

She quickly spun around at her name being called and almost fell back down the stairs doing so. Shining her light down the stairs, she could see that no one was there. She had recognized the voice that had called her name as one of the twins. The problem was that she knew she had just heard giggling coming from somewhere upstairs, and now one of them was calling her back down the stairs. They were playing a game with her. *Fine! Let's play a game*, she thought to herself. Which one did she go after first, the one that had made the giggling sound upstairs where she was now, or go back downstairs to find the sister? Claire decided to take the upstairs first. She proceeded down the hallway where she had thought she had heard the giggling. She came upon a shut door that was most likely a bedroom. Claire tucked her flashlight in her armpit so the light still would shine at the door. Then she used that hand to slowly turn the door handle while her other hand kept her gun aimed at the door. Claire shoved the door inward. As the door flung open, Claire caught sight of someone pointing a gun at her. In a panic, she fired two shots from her revolver. Glass shattered and hit the ground shattering even more. Claire shined her light again at the target only to see what she shot was the bathroom mirror. It was her own reflection that she had seen. Heart pounding in her chest and feeling like an idiot, Claire leaned heavily on the door frame. Then all of a sudden, she heard gunshots, many of them ringing out in the distance.

"John!" Claire blurted, remembering Sallie Mae's message earlier. Claire immediately started back down the hallway and back down the stairs. Rushing to John's aid, she almost made it to the front door.

"Don't go, Claire!" came a voice from somewhere down below her. "Lisa and Lucy want to play!" came another voice. "Lisa and Lucy will make you pay!" came the first voice again.

It was the twins, and both of them were somewhere below her, most likely in the basement. Claire stood there for a moment, torn between going to help John or taking care of these little bitches. Claire opted for the latter. She went toward where the calls had come from, again with a flashlight in one hand and her revolver in the other. Off to the side of the kitchen was an open door. Claire shined her light in and saw it was stairs leading to the basement. She started down the stairs a couple of steps before stopping suddenly. Remembering that Edith had fallen down the stairs most likely due to a tripwire the twins had set up, Claire pointed her flashlight down at the stairs and there it was, about two more steps down. A fishing line had been tied to the poles in the railings waiting for unsuspecting prey to fall for the trap. Not Claire, though. She wasn't going to fall for the same trap others had. She carefully stepped over the fishing line onto the next step below the trap, one foot at a time.

"You are going to have to do a lot better than that!" Claire shouted into the darkness below her. Smiling, she started down the stairs again. But then the steps gave way, and she was soon falling.

***

John kissed her passionately while grabbing her and pulling her into him.

Welcoming the embrace, Claire kissed him passionately back. How much she loved him. How well did she always feel in his arms? John slowly pulled back from her so he could look into her eyes. At first, he looked at her like she was everything in the world. She liked the way he looked at her. But then, a look of concern spread across his handsome face. Gently he reached up to the side of Claire's head as if to move her hair out of her face. When John pulled his hand back, it was covered in blood. Panicking, Claire tried to reach up and touch her head, which now hurt painfully. However, to her surprise and horror, she couldn't move her hands! In fact, the more she tried, something cut into her wrists. Claire suddenly opened her eyes to see a room lit by candlelight. There was no John; she was alone.

She was on her side, and the side of her head was lying in something wet. A sharp pain shot through her head, causing her to once again reach for it, but the act only caused more pain in her wrists. That's when Claire realized that her hands were bound by something, something that cut deep into her wrists when she tried to move them. Claire then tried to move her feet, but as she already suspected, they were also bound. The twins must have figured she would have seen the tripwire and stepped over it. They must have rigged the steps after the one the tripwire had been on to fall under her weight. So stupid of her to think she had outsmarted the twins. The laugh the girls must have had as she had come crashing down, Claire thought to herself. Claire knew she had to be in the basement and took a look around to get her bearings. There were candles all over, and their many tiny flames gave enough light to see while casting disturbing shows along the walls and ceiling.

Claire tried to lift her head and almost passed out again from the pain that radiated through her. Claire vomited from sudden nausea that came over her but managed to maintain her consciousness.

"Oh! You are awake!" came the familiar voice of one of the twins.

Claire arched her back and tilted her head in the direction of the voice. Her eyes shot wide open when she was able to see where the voice had come from. There, standing before her, were both the twins looking even scarier in the candlelight. But it wasn't the sight of the twins that had her staring wide-eyed. It was what was behind them. There, just behind the twins, was a makeshift altar. On top of the altar was a decaying pig's head, Betsy's decaying pig's head. Claire wanted to scream out in horror. She wanted to break free of the restraints. She wanted to grab each twin by their little necks and watch their faces as she squeezed their very life from them.

"Don't worry, Claire. Betsy is in a better place now," said Anna, seeing Claire's eyes open wide at the sight of Betsy's head.

"Betsy is happy," chimed in Anabel

"Betsy is now with Mommy and Daddy in Heaven," said Anna.

"And Grandma said that's where everyone is happy," said Anabel.

"Yes, and soon Grandma will soon be with Grandpa," finished Anna.

Claire's heart stopped beating for a minute, for there it was, they had killed Earl! For all her valiant efforts, Earl still died. Not only that, but John was now probably dead, and soon so would she. What bothered her even more than her emanate death was that these little girls were still going to kill poor Edith and get away with all of it.

"I hope you bitches rot in Hell!" Claire spat in defiance. "Oh no, Hell is for very bad people," replied Anna.

"Yes, Hell is for bad people and sacrifices," said Anabel.

"Lisa and Lucy say that is where we are to send you," said Anna. Both girls then held out their dolls to Claire as if that was all the explanation she needed.

"Listen, those dolls aren't real," began Claire, remembering what John had said about the darkness and objects. Claire thought she might have a way to reason with the girls. "John said the dolls are just an outlet because you don't know how to deal with your emotions. The dolls allow uncontrolled emotions to turn into darkness. Don't you see that? You girls weren't like this until you got the dolls. I have seen the difference in old pictures of you. You have to get rid of those dolls, and you will be alright again. No one else needs to get hurt."

"Lisa and Lucy say that John is darkness itself, and one day it will consume him completely if it already hasn't," responded Anna.

"Lisa and Lucy keep us from that darkness," said Annabel.

"That is why you and John have to be sacrificed," said Anna.

"It will help Lisa and Lucy protect us," said Annabel.

"You both are insane!" cried Claire in hopeless defiance.

The twins' spreading smile was truly horrifying in the candlelight. Just then, a truck's engine could be heard pulling up the driveway outside. Both girls quickly looked at each other rather than at Claire.

"Help! I am down here!" screamed Claire with all her might. Anna quickly closed the distance between her and Claire, raised her foot, and stomped down hard on Claire's head.

***

Ravenclaw pulled up to the Claymores' driveway, stopping right next to Claire's cruiser. Sallie Mae had gotten a hold of the Warden after getting no response from anyone, including Claire. She told the Warden about Claire's cryptic message that it was the twins and that she was at the Claymore's house. Then she told the Warden there was also the possibility of trouble brewing between Deputy Jones and John. At first, the Warden didn't know which place to go first until Sallie Mae mentioned that she could no longer get a hold of Claire. Sallie Mae told the Warden that she was deeply worried about her, so he had decided to check on Claire first. Like Claire, the Warden figured that John could take care of himself. Now, seeing the Claymores' house completely dark, Claire's cruiser with its lights still on, and the front door hanging wide open, he was thinking that he had made the right decision. The Warden jumped out of his truck and then grabbed a flashlight and his machete that he often used to clear brush out of the back seat. The Warden took a different approach than Claire, though. He decided not to go in from the front of the house and announce his presence. Instead, the Warden went around to the back of the house to where a set of double doors led down into the cellar, which led to the basement. If something bad was truly happening inside the house, he wanted to catch whatever it was by surprise and not the other way around.

The moon was bright enough that he didn't need to use his flashlight just yet, which gave him some advantage in being stealthy. The Warden found the double doors to the cellar unlocked and made his way inside. The Warden left double doors open to allow some of the moonlight to come inside, which the Warden then used to navigate around the stacked boxes of old junk. He saw some faint light coming from an archway across from him and made his way silently toward it. The Warden cautiously approached the wall next to the open archway and put his back against it. He stayed there for a moment listening for anything that might indicate if someone was around the corner. He heard nothing, so he cautiously peeked around the corner into the room. At first, the Warden didn't believe what his eyes were seeing. There were lit candles spread all over the room among the collected junk.

In the back of the room was some kind of crude altar with candles lined around something big and apparently rotting. The scene before the Warden was like something out of a horror movie. Then the Warden's eyes went wide when he realized that the rotting thing surrounded by the candles was Betsy's Head. The Warden started forward when a groan came from somewhere on the side of him. Startled by the sound, the Warden raised his machete to strike at whatever made the noise. However, when the Warden saw that it was Claire, he ran to her and dropped down to his knees. He laid his machete and flashlight on the ground behind him. Then, he gently lifted Claire's head in his hands. She was unconscious and blood-soaked on one side of her head. The Warden could make out a wicked-looking gash on the bloodied side. He started to move Claire, but she moaned in pain, causing him to stop. Gently, the Warden set her head back on the ground and carefully rolled her onto her side. He then reached back and grabbed his flashlight then shined it onto Claire's wrists. Claire's wrists were also covered in blood. They were bound with something that was cutting deeply into them. It was a fishing line! Someone had bound her hands with a fishing line! *Exactly what the hell was going on?* the Warden thought to himself. Pulling out his pocket knife, he carefully cut the line as best as he could without causing any more injury to Claire. After he got her hands free, he started on the line that also was binding her legs. He had just freed Claire's legs when Claire started coming to.

"What?" asked Claire groggily while trying to open her eyes. The pain in her head was worse than before.

"Claire, it's David Ravenclaw. Who did this to you?" asked the Warden earnestly.

"Raven-claw?" slurred Claire.

"Yes, it's me, David," the Warden assured her as he leaned closer to her face so she could see better.

Seeing Claire squinting hard at him, the Warden took his flashlight and shined the light onto his own face so she could get a better look. It worked, the

THE TWINS

Warden saw Claire's eyes pop open in recognition, and a smile of relief started to form on her bloodied face.

Then the Warden saw Claire's eyes pop open even wider at something behind him. He quickly turned around only to see his machete coming down on the side of his exposed neck. The blade bit deep enough to sever the carotenoid artery. As the wielder of the machete ripped the blade free, blood shot out of the Warden's neck like a fountain showering everything, including Claire, who was now screaming. The Warden tried to clamp down on the wound with his hands to try and stop his life's blood from leaving him. However, all his actions did was make the blood shoot out between his fingers. He tried to get to his feet, but another blow from the machete came down on the hand that was clutching his wounded neck. The machete cut into the Warden's hand, severing a couple of fingers. He let out an agonizing scream as his severed fingers fell to the ground. Then something hard slammed him across the head opposite the side from his neck wound. The blow was hard enough to drive him all the way to the ground immobilizing him. All the Warden could do was lay there helpless and watch his blood flow freely onto the floor while waiting for the final blow that would finish him off.

Claire couldn't stop herself from screaming as she watched both Anna and Anabel's continued attacks on the poor helpless Warden. Despite the pain in her head, wrists, and legs, Claire tried to get up and run. But as she tried to climb to her feet, she kept slipping on the blood-covered floor. Desperate, Claire started crawling like a worm toward the only exit she could see in the candlelight, the one archway that the Warden must have entered from. At first, she made very little progress, but then she was able to slowly inch her way forward. Each time Claire heard the sickening wet splat or thud sound still going on behind her, it gave her the power to push on. Finally, as Claire found dryer flooring that allowed more traction, she got to her hands and knees. She was about to put all her energy into one final burst to get to her feet and run, but then she noticed that the wet splat and thud sounds had stopped. Claire slowly turned her head and looked over her shoulder. There, standing right behind her, were Anna and Anabel. Anna had the machete in one hand and her doll in the other. Anabel held a baseball bat in one hand and her doll in the other.

Both girls were covered in blood, which made the sight truly horrifying in the candlelight.

"Sorry about your friend," said Anna, completely devoid of all emotion.

"But he ruined Lisa and Lucy's game," said Anabel.

"He was supposed to come in through the front door," said Anna.

"He was supposed to play the game by the rules," said Anabel.

"Instead, he broke the rules," said Anna.

"He came in from the cellar," said Anabel.

"And ruined our game," said Anna.

"So, he had to pay," said Anabel.

"Now it is your turn," said Anna.

"To pay," finished Anabel.

"Stop!" cried Claire, falling back to the floor, knowing that it was hopeless now. "Just stop."

"We can't stop," said Anna as she raised her machete high overhead to prepare for a strike.

"We can't be stopped," said Anabel as she raised her bat overhead like her sister. "For nothing can stop the light!" the twins exclaimed in unison.

"*Darkness* can," came a hiss from the other side of the darkened archway. Both twins looked up to see John slowly step out of the shadows into the candlelight. For the first time, Claire saw fear in those dark pools of the twin's eyes.

"No!" screeched the twins, who then charged at John.

Unknown to the twins, it wasn't John the girls charged at. It was the *Darkness,* and it was quicker. The *Darkness* brought up his gun and rapidly fired two shots. Both shots found their mark between each of the twin's eyes, blowing large holes out the back of each of their heads while flinging their bodies back to the floor. The *Darkness* walked slowly over to the twin's bodies and stood over them. Just then, something caught the *Darkness's* eyes, and it looked up to see Betsy's rotting head on the crude altar. The *Darkness* fired two more shots into each of the twins' chest cavities without taking his eyes off Betsy's head.

Claire watched it all happen, with many different emotions running through her all at once. But the greatest emotion she felt right then as she watched the *Darkness* fire shots into the dead twin's bodies was fear. She feared that the *Darkness* had finally won, just like the twins had warned. However, when it turned back to face her, she saw it was John and that the *Darkness* was gone. John then rushed over to Claire and picked her up into his arms, holding her close to his chest. As John clutched Claire tightly, he staggered into a stack of old boxes, knocking some of them over. Now that John was back in control, the gunshot wounds and a large amount of blood loss he had suffered started to take their toll. Claire looked up into John's deep blue eyes, concerned. He just smiled.

"Promise me we'll never have kids," Clarie said. She saw John nod his head before she fell unconscious again.

***

The lit candle rolled across the floor after being knocked to the ground by the boxes John had bumped into. The tiny flame caught hold of some old rags in the corner and started to grow. As the flame grew, it started to rapidly spread around the room. Soon the Claymores' entire house was up in flames. A house that was handcrafted and passed down from generation to generation was now a raging inferno.

Epilogue

Claire slowly opened her eyes and saw the ceiling of the hospital room. The pain in her head was gone. In fact, she didn't feel any pain at all. She looked at her wrists which were now heavily bandaged with a little blood soaking through.

"So the hero is awake," came a voice to Claire's side, startling her. Claire turned her head toward the voice, and there was Detective Marshal sitting in a chair off to the side in a corner. He had an unlit cigarette hanging in the corner of his mouth. As Claire looked at him, he took the cigarette out of his mouth and gave her a gentle smile.

"What happened?" Claire asked. Her mind and her memory were a little fuzzy at the moment. She raised her hand to her head and found that it was bandaged up pretty good.

"Well, it looks like you tried to take on the twins of Satan by yourself. Which probably wasn't the best idea, by the way, since you almost died last night due to that nasty head injury. You lost a lot of blood. In fact, if whatever your hands were bound with had cut any further into your wrist, you most likely wouldn't have made it," replied the Detective.

"The twins!" Claire exclaimed, her memories all coming back. She tried to get up and out of the hospital bed, but the Detective was immediately by her side, easing her back down.

"It's alright. They won't be killing anyone anymore," assured the Detective. Claire still gave him a doubting look. "After John carried you out of the Claymores' house, it caught fire and burned completely to the ground, apparently with the twins inside."

"John!" Claire exclaimed. Again she tried to get up.

"He is fine now, resting in a room down the hall," replied the Detective as he once again eased Claire back down. "Although, it was a little touch and go there for a while for him as well. Your friend had sustained a couple of gunshot wounds to the abdomen and lost a lot of blood as well.

"Travis, is he...?" Claire began.

"Dead? Yes. It looks like your Deputy and his two buddies bit off more than they could chew. We found all three of their bodies at Mr. Colt's trailer," replied the Detective. A chill ran through the Detective just then as he remembered seeing the carnage at the trailer. The scene resembled something out of a war movie. Then there was the cold efficiency in the way the Deputy and his buddies were taken out. The Detective knew those images were going to haunt him in his nightmares for a very long time.

"How did you know how to find them?" Claire asked, confused. Hell, how did the Detective know about what had happened? Why was he here? Claire thought to herself.

"After you humiliated me and stormed out of my office, a beat cop by the name of Officer Miller came into my office. He had seen you exit and told me all about the hospital incident and the warrant for Mr. Colt," started the Detective. Seeing Claire give a start at the mention of the warrant, the Detective waved it off with a smile. "Don't worry, Mr. Colt is not going to be arrested."

"I don't understand," said Claire, still confused.

"After I was told by Officer Miller about the hospital incident, I went to the hospital and had them go through all the security footage around the time of the murder. This time instead of focusing on Mr. Colt, we focused on the twins. There was one video angle that barely caught it, but it did show the twins going into Tobi Harnet's hospital room. They left a right after Mr. Harnet's vitals flatlined. The video and all the other evidence, including the ones you so kindly pointed out to me, clear your boyfriend," explained the Detective. Claire breathed a sigh of relief. "After that, I tried to get ahold of you but got your dispatcher Sallie Mae, who then filled me in on your and Mr. Colt's situation.

For the first time in a long time, Claire finally felt that the nightmare was over, and she visibly relaxed. She closed her eyes and soon was fast asleep. The Detective pulled the blankets up to Claire's chin to make sure she would be warm and comfortable. He quietly walked to the door and opened it. He took one last look at this remarkable woman.

"Rest easy, Hero. It is all over. You are safe now," whispered the Detective, then he turned and left.

THE TWINS

A couple of hours later, Claire woke up to find herself alone in her hospital bed. There came a soft knock at the door, and then a nurse popped in. The nurse, who looked like the grandmotherly type, greeted Claire as she started checking Claire's bandages. A second knock soon came, and the nurse went over to open the door. There was John in a wheelchair. He had a tube running from his arm to an I.V. that was hooked onto a metal rolling rack behind him.

There was a very large male nurse behind John that started pushing John and his I.V. into the room as the other nurse welcomed them both in. The male nurse wheeled John around to Claire's side; then, he excused himself, saying that he would be back shortly to get John. John reached out and took Claire's hand into his own. Claire instantly felt a warmth come over her, and she smiled lovingly at him. The two just stared at each other without saying a word. They didn't have to. Their eyes said everything they needed to say. The nurse seeing the two of them having a moment, politely excused herself, but neither Claire nor John heard her or noticed as she left the room.

"You came for me," Claire said, finally breaking the long silence.

"I will always come for you," John whispered. "Never doubt that. Nothing will ever stand in my way."

Tears rolled freely down Claire's cheeks. All her emotions coming to her at once, Claire shook uncontrollably. John got up out of the wheelchair and ripped the IV from his arm. He climbed into the bed beside Claire and pulled her close. He could feel her immediately calm down. He tilted her head up so their eyes could meet once again. He leaned down and kissed her, and she welcomed it.

***

The wheels squeaked every so often as the caregiver pushed the wheelchair down the near-empty hallway. The elderly woman sitting in the wheelchair stared vacantly as she was wheeled past all the other resident's rooms in the assisted living facility. The hallways were relatively quiet at this time of the night except for a few other residents that were also going to their rooms to get ready for bed. The caregiver pushing the elderly woman was a very large, powerful-looking woman. Although her appearance was intimidating to many who

THE TWINS

first saw her, she had a very gentle soul, and it showed in how well she cared for all the residents. Her gentleness really came out when she took care of the elderly woman she was now pushing. The caregiver couldn't explain it, but whenever she was put in charge of the elderly woman, she felt happy. The elderly lady never really said anything, only mumbled the same phrase from time to time, but there was something about her that was warming.

"Alright, Edith, we are home, let's get you ready for bed," said the caregiver as she opened the door to Edith's room and wheeled her inside. The room was relatively large and spacious. In one corner, there was a large oak dresser that looked like it was handcrafted. Some little tables were strategically placed around the room as well. On top of the dresser and tables sat some photos that the caregiver assumed had once been Edith's friends and family. She loved looking at the photos when she came to Edith's room because the people in them always looked happy and filled with love. Well, all of them except the one photo that had a man, a woman, and twin girls in it. In that photo, the man and woman were holding hands while looking at each other lovingly. The twin girls' expressions, however, were totally the opposite.

The caregiver couldn't accurately describe the girls' expressions exactly, but they always sent a shiver down her spine, giving her the creeps. The caregiver helped Edith out of the wheelchair and onto the bed. Once on the bed, the caregiver removed Edith's clothes and then dressed her in her nightgown. Finally, she tucked Edith in and made sure everything was just right. "Alright, Edith, you are set for bedtime. Is there anything else I can do for you before I go?" she asked. She knew that Edith never asked for anything, but she always wanted to make sure.

"Lisa and Lucy want to play. Lisa and Lucy will make you pay," replied Edith. It was the same reply Edith always gave, so the caregiver wasn't surprised when Edith said it.

She turned off the lights as she left the room and gently closed the door behind her. The only light in the room came from the night light beside Edith's bed, casting an eerie shadow on the ceiling.

"Yes, Lisa and Lucy will make them all pay," giggled Edith as she drifted off to sleep.

THE TWINS

***

The station wagon pulled into the gas station, coming to a stop at the gas pumps. The family inside the wagon had been traveling for a long time without seeing a gas station and figured it was best to top off the tank before they continued on with their vacation. Richard Novack and his wife Emily, along with their twin daughters, Susie and Sarah, had been waiting all year for their cross-country road trip. They had to miss last year's trip due to Richard's job, and he planned to make it up to his family this year. As Richard got out to fill up the tank, his wife noticed a small gift shop sitting off to the side of the gas station.

"Honey, I am going to take the girls and go check out that gift shop. Honk when you are ready to go," Emily said as she got out of the car and opened the back door for the girls to get out.

The girls were eager to get out and run around. They rushed out of the car as soon as Emily opened the door. Shutting the car doors, Emily grabbed the girls' hands and started for the gift shop. The store was very plain and in a very bad need of a paint job. There were no other signs on the building except for the fading one saying Gift Shop. A beaded curtain was hanging in the entranceway, which the twin girls ran eagerly through, screaming and laughing. Emily came in after them and saw that the gift shop looked more like everyone had taken all their old garage sale items and dumped them there. Emily didn't mind too much, though. She had often found some real gems in someone else's trash. The twins immediately went to the area in the store that housed all the toys and dug right in. As Emily looked at some of the antique items, she saw an elderly woman behind the counter. The lady was dressed up like a gypsy, with a multicolored flowing dress and a colorful scarf wrapped around her head. The lady's outfit was completed with dangling cosmic earrings and gaudy rings on every finger.

"Good afternoon," Emily offered with a smile.

"Would you like your palm read? Only fifteen dollars," responded the old lady in a raspy voice.

"Thank you, but I am good for now," Emily politely declined.

"Ten dollars?" countered the old lady.

"Again, thank you, but maybe another time," Emily gently declined again and then proceeded to walk away.

"Five dollars, final offer!" the old lady persisted.

"Really, I am good. My daughters and I were just leaving," replied Emily, starting to tire of the game.

As Emily started walking away, the old lady suddenly reached out and grabbed Emily's hand. Emily tried to pull her hand away from the old lady's grip, but the old lady's grip was like a vice. She turned Emily's palm up so she could inspect it. Then all of a sudden, the old lady released Emily's hand and shrank back.

"What is it? What did you see?" Emily asked, clutching her hand to her chest. But the old lady just shook her head and shrank back further.

"Mommy! Look what Sarah and I found!" exclaimed a very excited Susie. Both Sarah and Susie held up the two dolls they had found in the pile of toys at the back of the store. Both dolls were in very bad shape. They both looked like they had been in a fire because they were covered with burn marks. One doll particularly looked bad because it had what looked like a fishing line holding its head and arm on.

"Can we keep them, please, Mommy?" begged Sarah.

"I don't know, girls, we still have a lot of traveling, and there are other things you might want more," replied Emily, who was still absently rubbing her hand.

"Please, Mommy!" exclaimed Susie.

"We will be good," chimed in Sarah.

"We won't ask for anything else," said Susie. Both girls were now picking up speed as they picked up where the other one finished.

"This is all we want!" said Sarah.

"Please give us this one thing!" said Susie.

"Ok, ok, alright, you can have them!" exclaimed Emily, exhausted by the twin's rapid-fire pleas. Since when did they start doing that? Emily thought to herself. Turning around to the old lady, Emily asked, "How much for the dolls?"

"Nothing, take them." replied the old lady, who seemed to actually shrink as she moved to the furthest spot behind the counter.

"I'm sorry?" asked Emily uneasily, not understanding what was happening.

"I don't want your money, take the dolls and begone," said the old lady, shooing them with her hands to leave her store.

"I just take the dolls without paying for them?" Emily asked.

"BEGONE!" shrieked the old lady.

Emily and the twins jumped as they were startled by the screeching old woman. Emily immediately grabbed the twins by their arms and practically ran out of the store all the way back to the car. Richard was just getting into the car as Emily, and the twins came running up.

"Something wrong?" Richard asked, noticing that Emily and the girls looked scared. Emily didn't say anything. She just opened the back car door and shuffled the girls in.

Then she got into the car and locked the door. Richard got into the car and shut his door, giving Emily a questioning look.

"We need to leave now," Emily responded.

"What's wrong? You're scaring me," Richard asked, very worried by Emily's weird behavior.

"Nothing. Can we just go, please?" Emily asked, almost pleading.

Richard gave Emily and the girls one more concerned look before starting the car. An hour later, they were all driving down the road with the gift shop and the creepy old woman long behind them. The twins, playing with their dolls, were very content and started to sing.

"Lisa and Lucy want to play. Lisa and Lucy will make you pay."

To Ally,
Thanks for
Being great!!

Made in the USA
Columbia, SC
20 August 2022